Scottish
Bakehouse
Mysteries™

Quill the Messenger

Elizabeth Penney

Annie's®
AnniesFiction.com

Books in the Scottish Bakehouse Mysteries series

Library of Congress-in-Publication Data
Quill the Messenger / by Elizabeth Penney
p. cm.
I. Title

2020947305

AnniesFiction.com
(800) 282-6643
Scottish Bakehouse Mysteries™
Series Creator: Shari Lohner
Series Editor: Elizabeth Morrissey
Cover Illustrator: Kelley McMorris

10 11 12 13 14 | Printed in South Korea | 9 8 7 6 5 4 3 2

1

Molly Ferris smiled as her Scottish terrier scampered around the backyard, pausing to investigate every enticing aroma. Angus was overjoyed that warm weather had come to Loch Mallaig, Michigan—and so was she. Seasons often changed a bit later in Michigan's Upper Peninsula, but it was always worth the wait. Now it was May, and the trees were in full leaf, birds sang and soared overhead, and the warmth of the rising sun promised a lovely day ahead.

Stretching her arms wide, Molly inhaled fresh, sweet air. In this beautiful but cold corner of the country, each and every sunny day was something to cherish. Although it was the busy season for Bread on Arrival, the Scottish bakehouse she co-owned with two partners, she tried to spend plenty of time outdoors. Having a small but active dog who needed regular walks certainly helped with that goal.

A glance at her phone informed her that time had flown by and she needed to head back into the bakery. Fortunately, Molly lived in an apartment above it, so she didn't have far to go to take Angus home. Molly clapped her hands. "Angus, come."

Head baker Laura Donovan was already inside the kitchen with the ovens going, and their third partner, Carol MacCallan, was pulling into the driveway. As Molly began herding her reluctant pet toward the outside staircase to her apartment, Carol got out of her car.

"Gorgeous day, isn't it?" Carol called. Tote in one hand and purse in the other, she used her hip to shut the car door.

"It sure is," Molly said. "After I put Angus in, I'll be right down."

"See you in a few." Carol took the path that led to the staff entrance of the bakehouse, which was a pale yellow Victorian trimmed with black shutters.

Molly got Angus inside and settled, then unlatched the doggy door that led to the yard and promised him another walk later that morning during a lull at the bakehouse. Then she washed up, tied on an apron, and hurried down the interior stairs, eager for a cup of coffee and a sample of whatever delight Laura had dreamed up today.

At the bottom of the stairs, she came face-to-face with famous romance cover model Gregory Gregg. Or at least a life-size cutout of him, dressed in his trademark kilt, sandy hair flowing and brawny arms bare. Molly yelped and jumped backward.

Laura and Carol laughed. "She got me with that too," Carol said. "He was right by the back door when I came in."

Molly grabbed the cardboard Gregory by the shoulders and moved it aside. "Where did you get this?"

"A bookstore in Marquette." Laura slid her hands into oven mitts. "They were going to throw it away so I grabbed it. I thought it would be fun to have around since Castleglen is hosting that Scottish historical romance conference this week."

"Fergus told me Gregory Gregg is supposed to be here in the flesh," Molly said, then blushed. Her good friend Fergus MacGregor, the handsome owner of the Castleglen golf resort, had teased her lightly about the model being in town, and it had given her an odd feeling at the time. "Lots of best-selling Scottish romance authors are doing workshops and signings too."

"And don't forget the high tea we're catering." Carol handed Molly a mug of coffee. "Try a maple walnut scone." She pointed to a tray of tiny frosted scones sprinkled with pieces of nuts.

Molly didn't wait for a second invitation. She picked up the scone and bit into it eagerly. The treat melted in her mouth. The frosting, made with locally produced maple syrup, gave a sweet and satisfying burst of flavor. "Oh Laura, these are going to disappear in two seconds flat."

"I've got a few other flavors." Laura pulled another tray of scones out of the oven. "I'm doing bite-size versions so people can try more than one."

"Guess what?" Carol asked, snagging a scone for herself. "Laura found a source of early season rhubarb and is making strawberry-rhubarb tarts too."

"Oh, I adore strawberry rhubarb. It's one of my favorite combinations." Molly took her first sip of fresh-brewed coffee, one of her favorite morning moments. "You're on fire today, Laura." Actually the baker was on fire every day, consistently turning out delectable and creative baked goods. Tourists often said that they'd heard about the bakehouse from friends or relatives, which meant their reputation was spreading.

Laura, who was setting scones on a rack to cool, smiled modestly. "I try. Changing the subject, we're still going over to the conference after we close, right?"

"Definitely." Carol pointed to her tote, which was resting under the coatrack. "I grabbed every Madelaine Alt book I own for her to sign."

"Hasn't she written about thirty books?" Molly knew that fans lined up for blocks whenever the famous author held a book signing, and she was often a featured guest at conferences like the one this week. Millions of her books were in print.

"Yes, she has," Carol said. "And I own twenty-nine of them." She chuckled ruefully. "Mostly in paperback, of course, since my book budget isn't huge."

"Do you think they'll be selling her books at the conference?" Molly asked. "I don't have any, but it would be fun to get one signed."

"Of course." Laura stacked the empty tray to be washed. "There will be tons of books to buy and all kinds of other merchandise." She smiled. "I've had myself on a budget for weeks so I could splurge on this."

"The vendor area is going to be great." Carol sighed in delight. "I even made a list of the booths I want to visit."

Molly went to the coffee maker and poured herself a refill. "I'm looking forward to the classes we signed up for."

"Herbal teas, bonnet trimming, and love letter writing," Carol recited, then grinned. "Complete with quills."

"I've never written with a quill," Molly said with a laugh.

"Me neither, but I'm sure it'll be fun," Carol said, bringing her mug over so Molly could fill it.

"I think so too." Laura added more flour to her mixing bowl. "But in the meantime, we've got a lot to do."

"I'll help you bake after Bridget comes in at eight," Carol said.

"Perfect." Laura glanced at the clock. "We open in ten."

Molly and Carol kicked into gear, finishing their coffee and heading to the front of the bakehouse to take care of a few pre-opening tasks. Then, at opening time on the dot, Molly unlocked the door and flipped the sign to *Open*.

Cars began to pull into the lot and for the next little while, they ran to pour hot beverages and serve fresh baked goods to their customers. Molly was restocking mugs during a lull when a middle-aged woman walked in, alone. Her first thought was that she seemed familiar, with her silvery bob hairstyle and lean features. Her skin was lightly tanned, and she had green eyes behind a pair of trendy eyeglasses.

Then Molly recognized her and yelped, "Patsy Mae Wallace! What are you doing here?"

Molly set down the tray of mugs and bolted around the counter to greet the newcomer, a friend the Bakehouse Three had made in college more than thirty years earlier. Carol followed on Molly's heels, also exclaiming in surprise and delight.

Patsy Mae returned their fervent hugs. "Oh my, this is quite a welcome," she said, her charming Southern accent a nod to her Louisiana roots.

"Laura, get out here," Carol called. "You'll never guess who's here."

A moment later, Laura appeared from the kitchen, wiping her hands on a towel. Her face lit up. "Patsy Mae, I was just thinking about you." She exchanged a hug with her old friend.

"Good things, I hope," Patsy Mae said with a laugh.

"You bet," Laura replied. "You must be in town for the conference."

Seeing Patsy Mae's cheeks redden, Molly wondered what was going on. "Are you a big Scottish romance fan?"

"She's more than that," Laura said proudly. "She's an author."

Laura's announcement had drawn attention from other customers, deepening Patsy Mae's blush. "Hush now, Laura. I'm only an aspiring author. That's why I'm here, to try to connect with literary agents and editors."

"That's amazing." Carol took her friend's elbow and steered her toward the counter. "Let's get you something to eat and drink. Then you can fill us in."

Patsy Mae took a few minutes to admire the offerings on hand, then chose black coffee and a cream scone with lemon curd. "I'll have to come in every day I'm here so I can try everything," she said.

"You'll get a chance to sample more of Laura's baking at the conference," Molly assured her, setting Patsy Mae's selections on a tray. "We're catering a tea and some of the sessions."

"Lucky us," Patsy Mae said, picking up the tray.

"Let's sit over there so I can keep an ear out for the timers," Laura said, pointing, and everyone followed her.

For the next little while, everyone got caught up on news, with Patsy Mae giving an update on her two grown children, Lauren and Jerome, and her work as a librarian.

At the jingle of the bell on the front door announcing new customers, Molly started to rise, but Bridget Ross came out of the kitchen at that moment to start her shift. The college student who worked at the bakehouse part-time handled the newcomers, then hurried over to the table occupied by her bosses.

"You'll never guess who I saw on my way here." Bridget waited a beat, then offered her trademark sunny smile. "Gregory Gregg."

"You mean Laura's cardboard cutout?" Molly asked with a laugh.

Bridget shook her head, her dark hair flying. "No. The real one. He was walking along the sidewalk with a woman, headed this way." She glanced at the counter, where someone was waiting. "Excuse me, I'd better get to work." She hurried off.

"Oh my." Patsy Mae's hand went to her cheek. "Gregory Gregg is coming here, you think?" She pulled out a compact and checked her lipstick. "I'm a huge fan."

"Who isn't?" Laura asked wryly. The timer rang and she hopped up from her chair. "That's my cue. Talk to you all in a few."

"Did you hear about the contest?" Patsy Mae was smoothing her already flawless hair. "The winner gets to have supper with Gregory."

"You mean at the conference?" Although Molly admired many celebrities, she wasn't exactly starstruck. They were still people after all, even if they were unusually attractive or talented.

"It's a raffle." Patsy Mae snapped her compact closed and tossed it into her handbag. "The entry fees will benefit a literacy charity."

"That's a great cause," Carol said. "Maybe I'll enter."

"Does Harvey get to tag along to dinner if you win?" Molly teased, picturing Gregory, Carol, and her husband dining together.

"He'd insist on it," Carol said with a laugh, then dropped her voice. "But mostly because he reads Scottish romances too on the sly. He claims it's because he finds them lying around the house, but I know he secretly enjoys the sword fights and the happily ever afters."

"You're lucky to have him," Patsy Mae said wistfully. She cradled her mug in both hands pensively. "It's already been five years since I lost Bo."

"It's been twelve for me since Kevin passed," Molly said softly, her heart going out to her friend. Becoming widowed, especially at a relatively young age, was hard. "You'll always grieve, but it eases over time." And in time, she might even find room for new possibilities. Not that Molly was *quite* there herself. But almost, especially when it came to Fergus. Her spirits lifted when she realized she would see him later at the conference.

"The support of friends makes all the difference," Patsy Mae said, then seemed to shake off her sadness. "After Bo passed, I desperately needed a new passion in life. And one day I was working at the library, checking in some of my favorite authors, and I wondered, could I write a book? Maybe even get it published?"

"So you went ahead and started writing," Carol said. "Good for you."

Patsy Mae's smile was both proud and bashful. "Yes. I've written three books so far, although none of them have sold yet. Laura and I connected on social media, and she's been so encouraging even though I'm shy about it."

That explained why Laura had already known about their old friend's new endeavor. And how like Laura to keep the information under wraps until the right time.

"You'll have to tell us all about your books," Molly said, genuinely interested.

"Especially the dreamy Highlanders," Carol added with a teasing grin. "Are they all modeled after Gregory Gregg?"

Patsy Mae's blush returned. "I will admit dreaming that he'd be the cover model for one of my books. He's the best in the business."

"Maybe winning dinner with him will help," Molly said. "Or if you don't win, perhaps you can talk to him at the conference. Tell him about your books."

"If they're ever published . . ." Patsy Mae's words trailed off. Her eyes widened as she grabbed Carol on the forearm. "Don't look, but guess who just walked in."

Naturally Carol turned around and Molly glanced toward the door as well. An attractive couple stood inside the entrance, taking in the bakehouse. As they started toward the counter, Molly studied them in what she hoped was an unobtrusive manner.

He was tall, with flowing hair and a chiseled face, wearing jeans and a leather jacket—the immediately recognizable Gregory Gregg. Other customers had also noticed him and were exchanging whispers and nudges.

The woman with Gregory was also striking, if somewhat over-shadowed by the male model, with long, dark locks held back by a headband and pale, elegant features. She wore leggings, an open sweater over a silk blouse, and leather booties.

An unusual silence descended, the entire bakehouse watching as Bridget waited on the pair. "I'd like a dozen scones," the woman said, either oblivious to the attention or used to it.

"What flavor?" Bridget asked. She named off six varieties.

"How about an assortment? Two of each." Order placed, the woman began speaking to her companion in a low voice. He tilted his head to listen.

"Who is that with Gregory?" Carol asked, curiosity plain on her face.

Patsy Mae leaned across the table to respond. "That's Alyssa Martin," she said in a loud whisper. "She's a top editor at Tartan and Lace."

"Tartan and Lace is one of the top Scottish romance publishers," Carol said for Molly's benefit. "They publish Madelaine Alt's books."

"*The* top publisher," Patsy Mae corrected. "That's why I . . ." Her words trailed off. A frown knit her brows as she worried at her bottom lip with her teeth, chewing off all her carefully applied lipstick. She set down her mug and pushed back her chair, then hesitated. "Maybe I should wait."

"To do what?" Molly asked. But when Patsy Mae shook her head, Molly didn't push. Instead, she peered into her mug and saw it was empty. "I'd better get back to work." More cars were pulling into the lot and Bridget would need help. Carol started to rise, but Molly waved her down. "Keep Patsy Mac company."

Bridget was ringing up Alyssa's order when Molly slipped behind the counter. She smiled in the general direction of the pair. The editor ignored her, but Gregory greeted her with a warm grin.

"Nice place you have here," he said, his voice a deep, rich rumble flavored with a bit of Scots' burr. "You came highly recommended."

"That's nice to know," Molly said, her face heating under the model's scrutiny. "We do our best." Her cheeks burned hotter at her tepid response. Why couldn't she think of something witty to say? The man was entirely too good-looking, plus he had that elusive thing called charisma.

Bridget offered the box of scones to Alyssa, but Gregory reached forward to take it. Swallowing a chuckle, Molly watched a pink flush creep into Bridget's cheeks when the model's hands brushed hers.

Alyssa offered a tight smile of thanks, then slipped her arm through Gregory's. "Ready?"

Molly thought she heard a collective sigh of disappointment

from the women in the room. Were Gregory and Alyssa an item? It appeared that way. The couple whispered to each other as they crossed the floor toward the door.

"Miss Martin," a voice called. "Miss Martin." Patsy Mae was charging across the room, waving a hand to get the editor's attention.

Alyssa set her jaw. She stopped walking and waited for Patsy Mae to reach them. "How can I help you?" she asked, her tone frigid. Molly wondered if it was her usual reaction to strangers flagging her down. Editors must frequently get accosted by aspiring authors and often at inopportune times.

Patsy Mae inhaled visibly. She stood with her fists clenched at her sides and determination on her face. "My name is Patsy Mae Wallace. I submitted a book to you last year. *His English Rose?*"

Alyssa made an abrupt, dismissive gesture. "We get thousands of submissions a year. I can't possibly keep track of them all." She huffed derisively. "Now, if you'll excuse me." The editor tugged at Gregory's arm and the pair swept out the door, which shut behind them with a jingle of the bell.

2

A brief silence fell over the bakehouse. Then, as if orchestrated, the customers burst into chatter and laughter again. Patsy Mae, however, stood in the center of the room, her face a mask of misery.

Carol came rushing up and put her arm around Patsy Mae. "That woman was downright rude to you. I'm shocked."

Patsy Mae forced out a laugh. "I'm not. She hasn't responded to my e-mails or phone calls. I'm probably blacklisted by her company."

"But why?" Molly asked, joining her friends. "You didn't do anything wrong, did you?" She really had no idea how the publishing industry worked.

"I should have waited," Patsy Mae said. "But when I saw her in person again—well, something came over me."

"Again?" Carol repeated. "You've met her before?"

Patsy Mae nodded. "At a conference last year. I pitched my novel to her during a one-on-one. She seemed so excited about it, I was sure she would publish it. Silly me, right? Then, after I finished it and sent it in, I never heard another peep."

Molly frowned. "That's horrible. To get your hopes up like that and then ignore you? Anyone would be upset."

"And she pretended that she didn't recognize you or your book," Carol pointed out. "That was obvious to me."

Patsy Mae's fingers twisted together. "That's not the worst of it. The main character in my book was based on a real ancestor of mine. She was a lady-in-waiting to the English princess who became Saint Margaret, Queen of Scotland."

"That sounds fascinating," Carol said.

"Hold on," Patsy Mae said. "There's more." She swallowed. "A few months ago, I saw an announcement about Madelaine Alt's new book. It features a lady-in-waiting to Queen Margaret."

Carol gasped. "Seriously? Did she copy your plot?"

"Maybe," Patsy Mae said miserably. "I find it hard to believe that it was a coincidence. It took some real digging to even learn about Lady Evelyn. And I cited my research sources in my letter. I hoped they would offer credibility to my story."

"You think Alyssa actually shared your book with another author?" Carol was aghast.

"You wouldn't think so, would you?" Patsy Mae shrugged. "But I also queried Caroline Callahan, Madelaine's agent, with my manuscript and synopsis. If Tartan and Lace offered to publish my book, I would need an agent to handle the deal for me."

Molly's chest tightened in anger on her friend's behalf. "So whether she got the tip from Caroline or Alyssa, Madelaine used your sources for herself."

"It appears that way." Patsy Mae made a helpless gesture. "I don't know what to do. I haven't read Madelaine's book yet to compare it. And even if she did plagiarize, I don't have money for a lawyer. And maybe she just stole the idea. You can't copyright an idea."

Carol patted Patsy Mae on the shoulder. "I don't know what we can do to help, but we'll think of something."

"We sure will," Molly said. "And maybe another publisher will take one of your books and you'll be a huge success."

Patsy Mae laughed. "I can hope, right?" She gave her friends a tentative smile. "I do want to ask you a favor. But please say no if it makes you uncomfortable."

"Anything, Patsy Mae," Carol said.

"Well," the writer said, her voice hesitant. "I do have a new book ready. But this time when I tell people about it, I want a witness."

"You mean, sit in on the meetings?" Molly asked. That didn't sound too difficult. "If the agents and editors won't mind, I don't."

"What will you tell them about why we're there?" Carol asked. "Just curious."

Patsy Mae's cheeks reddened. "I didn't think that far ahead. You're right, it might look odd. And I don't need any more hurdles than I already have."

"What if I pretend to be your assistant?" Molly asked. "I can even take notes."

A grin broke across Patsy Mae's face. "What a great idea! I'm usually so flustered in those meetings, I can never remember what anyone says. You're the best." She gave Molly and Carol hugs. "See you at the conference later?"

"Definitely," Carol said. "We're heading right over after we close to attend the high tea reception."

"Wonderful." Patsy Mae gestured toward her table. "I'll let you two get back to work while I finish my breakfast." She smiled. "It's absolutely delicious. It'll get the bad taste Alyssa Martin left right out of my mouth."

"Is that everything?" Carol asked later that afternoon, her arms full of bakery boxes destined for the high tea.

Laura glanced around the bakehouse kitchen. "I believe so. The resort is going to provide dishes, silverware, and napkins, so we're all set." She handed Molly a tote of trays and tiered stands, then picked up a second stack of boxes. "Now we just need to make it out to the hearse in one piece."

The trio carted their burdens out to the 1939 LaSalle hearse they used to make deliveries. The eye-catching vehicle had come with the property, a former funeral home whose previous vocation had inspired the name Bread on Arrival.

Molly deposited the tote in the back with a sigh of relief after a busy day that hadn't had many lulls. Fortunately, Angus had happily spent his afternoon in the yard greeting customers through the fence instead of going on a longer walk. "I can't wait to sit down. Even if it's only for the drive to the resort."

"You and me both," Carol said as she headed toward the passenger door. "I think half our customers today came from the conference."

"I think so too," Molly said, sliding into the driver's seat. "A lot of them had Scottish romance novels and totes advertising the conference."

"I bet lots of other businesses saw heavy traffic today since the tea is the first official event," Carol said. "It seems like everyone checked in at the resort, then came to town to check things out."

Laura finished arranging the boxes to her satisfaction, then she climbed into the front seat beside Carol. It was a tight fit, but they managed. "This is going to be fun." She laughed. "I can't wait to see Gregory Gregg in costume, for one thing."

Molly started the vehicle and put it into gear. "I have to admit that Patsy Mae's situation dampened my enthusiasm a bit." She and Carol had filled Laura in about the possible theft of Patsy Mae's book idea.

"Same here," Carol agreed. "I might not even ask Madelaine to sign my books now."

"I can understand that," Laura said. "But I'm trying to check my wrath since we don't know for sure what happened. I think we need to focus on helping Patsy Mae get published with someone else. She is really, really good."

"You've read her writing?" Molly asked.

"Some of it," Laura said. "She wanted my opinion on the first few chapters of the Lady Evelyn book. It opens when the future Queen Margaret and her companions are shipwrecked in Scotland on their way to the Continent. According to Patsy Mae's description, they end up in the court of King Malcolm, who married Margaret. Lady Evelyn finds romance with a handsome Highlander."

"It sounds wonderful," Carol said with a sigh.

Molly agreed. She often wished real life could be as sweet as a romance novel. "I can't wait to read Patsy Mae's books."

Laura held up crossed fingers. "And here's hoping a publisher will snap her up soon."

The route to Castleglen, located two miles from downtown, was short but pleasant, leading them along the town's namesake lake. Trees in full leaf, flower gardens, and green lawns showed the quaint little village of Loch Mallaig at its best. Molly opened the car window so she could enjoy the unseasonably warm breeze on her face and in her hair. Oh, how she enjoyed spring, especially one that leaped right into summer.

Molly slowed the vehicle as they approached the resort before navigating into an entrance marked by stone pillars. The winding drive led them to the main building, a majestic structure of timber and stone set on the waterfront. Smooth golf greens dotted with white carts and golfers extended in every direction, and rowboats and canoes floated on the loch's blue water.

"I love coming here," Carol said as Molly halted the hearse under the portico at the front lobby entrance. "I feel more relaxed already."

"Me too," Molly said, opening her door. Once they set up the baked goods, they would officially be off the clock and free to participate in the conference.

Laura hurried inside to retrieve a cart while Carol opened the hearse's back door. Molly double-checked her tote for the Bread on Arrival rack cards they were going to set out. Providing treats for the high tea was a great advertising opportunity for the bakehouse and, as the trio's marketing guru, she planned to maximize it. Fergus had promised that Bread on Arrival would be listed as a vendor in the conference program as well.

Rumbling wheels announced the return of Laura, who was joined by Fergus, handsome in kilt and jacket.

"Good afternoon, ladies," he said with a smile, then began helping transfer boxes and totes to the cart.

"You're dressed already?" Molly asked him, alarm tingeing her voice. Had she gotten the time wrong? She and Fergus were members of The Piping Yoopers, the local bagpiper group performing at the event. She'd brought her costume along and planned to change after they set up the tea since there was plenty of time—or so she had thought.

Fergus pulled at his kilt with a laugh. "I've been wearing this all day. You'll see why in a minute."

Once they entered the hotel and made their way to the conference, Molly understood what Fergus had meant. At least half the guests were dressed in historical or traditional costume, as befitted fans of Scotland's past. As a woman rustled past in a gorgeous green satin gown, hair piled high to reveal huge, glittering earrings, Molly felt distinctly underdressed in her dress slacks and summery top.

Carol rolled her eyes. "I didn't realize the tea was formal," she muttered. "My gown is at the cleaners."

Molly laughed, resolving to enjoy the passing parade. The fact that people so strongly identified with the books they loved was fascinating. If they couldn't actually live in the past, at least they could pretend, she supposed.

The ballroom was packed already, with guests standing in clusters or circulating around the room. The air was also quite warm, and when they passed under a vent, Molly noticed it was blowing tepid air. "Is the air-conditioning on?" she asked Fergus.

He glanced up at the vent, his brows knit in concern. "We've been having some trouble with the system, but I thought it was fixed." He made a face. "What a day for it to act up. The temperature is way above normal this afternoon, and as you can see, we have a full house."

"Isn't that always the way?" Molly mused sympathetically. If a heating or air-conditioning system acted up, it always seemed to happen at the worst possible time.

Fergus pivoted on his heel. "I'd better go check into it, if you don't mind."

"Of course not," Molly said. "I'll catch up with you later. At our performance, if not before."

Laura steered the cart toward the buffet tables located along a wall. Resort servers were setting up mostly cold, savory selections, as befitted the warm weather. Molly spotted stacks of smoked salmon sandwiches, an array of salads, platters of crudités and bite-size fruit, and a selection of hot canapés. Another table held hot and cold coffee and tea.

Working quickly, the women loaded serving tiers and trays with the miniature treats Laura had baked. Pots of clotted cream and jam went into ice provided by the resort. More than one guest wandered by to eye the choices, obviously eager to dig in.

Molly's mouth was watering too. "Save me a salmon sandwich," she said to Laura. "I might as well get changed for the Yooper performance before the tea begins."

But Laura wasn't listening. Molly followed her gaze to the ballroom doorway. Trumpets weren't playing a fanfare, but Molly imagined them anyway as Gregory Gregg stepped through, dressed in full tartan regalia. Alyssa Martin was on his arm, and she wore a red gown resembling one Molly had seen on a popular television show. If Alyssa was wearing *that* for the opening reception, how could she possibly top it at the closing ball?

The onlookers burst into applause, the thunderous sound echoing around the large room. Laura's face was alight with excitement.

Carol elbowed Molly gently. "Go change. I'll make you a plate. Laura seems a bit distracted."

Molly murmured a thank-you, then picked her way through the crowd, deciding as she went that it'd be wiser to exit through a side door rather than the main entrance, where Gregory and Alyssa were being swarmed. The alternate route led her past two women standing close together. One was thin and elegant, with a sleek helmet of brown hair, the other shorter and stout, with brassy blonde hair in loose curls.

As Molly sidled by, she realized who they were. Madelaine Alt was the dark-haired woman, and her agent, Caroline Callahan, was the blonde. She'd seen a picture of them together on the conference program. Was it Molly's imagination, or was the air distinctly chillier in the vicinity of the two literary icons? Both wore sour expressions, that much was true. But was she getting the wrong impression based on her preconceived notions from Patsy Mae?

She smiled and nodded, even murmured a hello. In return, they both stared at her. Rebuffed, Molly jerked her head back around. She'd gotten the message loud and clear—don't speak to Madelaine and Caroline unless spoken to. She shivered. How intimidated aspiring authors must feel around the two industry powerhouses. Molly was relieved she didn't have to deal with them.

Outside in the parking lot, Molly grabbed her outfit and bagpipes, then changed in the ladies' room off the lobby. By the time she was done, sweat had broken out on her brow, little droplets peppering her skin. A hand held toward the closest vent revealed that nothing at all was blowing out. Had the system completely broken down? She sure hoped not, for the sake of the conference.

Molly turned on a tap and splashed her face with cool water, then dried off with a paper towel. Hopefully there would be better airflow in the ballroom so the Yoopers wouldn't pass out while playing. It took quite a bit of energy and breath to make those bagpipes sing.

Molly had almost reached the closed doors to the ballroom when the light sconces along the wall began to flicker. The overhead lights glowed brighter before fading out entirely. Then with a clunk, the struggling hum of the air-conditioning ceased.

The power was out. And Molly was standing alone in the darkness.

3

Alarmed cries filled the air as the crowd inside the ballroom reacted to the blackout. Someone opened the door, but then shut it again when they realized the power was out in the corridor as well.

Molly froze in place, not quite sure what to do or where to go. It didn't make sense to proceed into the ballroom, where hundreds of people were milling around. Maybe she should head to the lobby, which was lit by large windows. Then she remembered that her phone had a flashlight app. She felt in her pocket and didn't find it, so set down her belongings to dig around in her bag.

The clanking of a tool belt, heavy footsteps, and the bouncing beam of a flashlight announced someone's arrival. A radio crackled. "I'm on my way, boss," a man said in a deep voice.

The beam of light moved and shone right into Molly's upturned face. She squinted and raised her hand to shield her eyes. "Ouch."

The beam moved quickly away. "I'm sorry, ma'am," the man said. "I didn't know anyone was out here."

Having finally found her phone, Molly rose to her feet. The man was tall and lean, well over six feet. She couldn't really see his features, but the light he held low revealed work boots and pants. He must be a Castleglen employee.

"Do you know what happened to the lights?" she asked.

"Not yet, but hopefully I can fix them soon," he said. "The generator should have kicked on, but for some reason it didn't. So I'm here to fetch Mr. MacGregor."

The ballroom door cracked open and a beam from a phone shone into the hallway. With a leap of her pulse, Molly recognized Fergus. "There you are, Reg," he said. "I take it the generator is acting up? It should have kicked in by now."

Reg shifted back and forth on his boots. "I'm afraid so. I thought you could work your magic on the old beast."

Fergus laughed. "I'll do my best. Hold on a second and I'll give our guests an update." Just before the door closed, his gaze fell on Molly. "What are you doing out here? Stranded in the dark?" He opened the door wider. "Come on in and find a seat."

Molly gratefully accepted his offer and gathered her belongings. She preceded him into the ballroom, then he led the way to where Carol and Laura were seated. All around the room, guests were using their phones as portable lights, and the staff had lit candles on the tables as well, creating a surprisingly cheery scene. Unfortunately, this was the resort's interior ballroom, so the large windows present in other meeting spaces were missing here.

Carol patted the empty chair beside her. "Have a seat, Molly. We were wondering when you'd get back."

His duty done, Fergus patted Molly on the shoulder then moved off. Molly set her bags down and slid onto the chair with a sigh of relief. "I was out in the hallway when the lights went out. It was nearly pitch-black out there, aside from the exit signs. No windows."

"That must have been scary," Laura said. "We were startled for a moment too. It happened so suddenly."

"Ladies and gentlemen," Fergus called from the front of the room. "We're very sorry about the inconvenience of losing power, but we'll soon have things right again. In the meantime, enjoy your tea." He paused. "If you can see it, that is."

Everyone laughed. Their charming host gave a wave and headed out the double doors to hopefully remedy the situation.

A bobbing beam announced the arrival of The Piping Yoopers leader Alastair Thomson, who was carrying his phone with the flashlight lit. In his seventies, Alastair was tall, with thick, white hair and mustache that nearly glowed in the darkness. "Glad to see you made it, Molly," he said. "I thought maybe you'd gotten lost in the dark."

"Almost did," Molly said, a little louder than usual because Alastair was somewhat hard of hearing. "But yes, I'm here and ready to play. When are we going on?"

Alastair glanced toward the ballroom entrance. "I think we'll wait until Fergus returns. We're down a member or two already, so we need him." His lips lifted in a wry smile. "If they don't get the lights back, we'll be performing by candlelight."

"I'd say it was in keeping with tradition," Carol put in. "Think of all those centuries before electricity."

Alastair nodded. "We can pretend we're in the eighteenth century."

Molly watched a man dressed in breeches saunter past, a white wig on his head. "Not hard to do with these costumes."

"Very true," Alastair agreed. He checked his phone. "Why don't we meet in fifteen minutes? Fergus should be back by then. We'll gather in our usual room off the corridor."

"See you then," Molly said. Once Alastair walked off, Molly turned her attention to the table. A plate of food held a salmon sandwich, vegetable sticks, berries, and a helping of pasta salad. She picked up the sandwich. "This looks great, Carol. Thank you."

"No problem," Carol said. "You must be starving. I was." She reached for a pitcher of iced tea to refill her own empty glass. "Would you like iced tea?"

"I'd love some." Molly held out her glass for Carol. Her throat was quite dry from the hot, stuffy air.

With almost an audible snap, the overhead lights and wall sconces came on bright and strong. The room erupted into cheers. In one corner, a woman Molly hadn't noticed began playing a harp, the rippling notes winding through the room. A vent overhead started to gust streams of lukewarm air, but Molly thought it was gradually getting cooler and hoped it wasn't wishful thinking on her part.

"Look," Laura said. "There's someone at the sign-in table. We can pick up our attendee packets now since we didn't have a chance earlier."

Molly swallowed the last of her smoked salmon sandwich, perfectly complemented by cream cheese and chives on a fresh baguette, and wiped her hands on a napkin. "Let's go now, before I need to meet The Piping Yoopers."

They were in line at the table when the double doors opened and Fergus and Reg walked in. They went over to the wall holding the thermostat, and Reg began playing with the controls.

"I haven't seen him around the resort before," Carol said, nodding toward Reg. "At first I thought he was one of the male models."

"Wrong outfit, at least for a Scottish romance convention," Laura said. "He's obviously a handyman."

Carol was still studying Reg. "He's not quite good-looking enough, though, is he? Male models are so handsome it's almost eerie."

The women whirled around when a male voice chuckled behind them. Gregory Gregg, tall and gorgeous and, yes, with an almost unearthly charisma, was standing close by. His blue eyes twinkled as he said, "Eerie. That's a new one on me."

"I'm sorry." Carol's hand flew to her mouth. "I didn't mean—"

"Don't worry about it, ma'am." The model waved off Carol's apology, then gestured to a small placard on the table. "I wanted to make sure that you sign up for the charity raffle." He winked. "Grand prize winner gets dinner with me."

When he turned to the next group of women to give the same message, Laura let out a sigh. "I wasn't going to sign up since Patsy Mae has her heart set on winning, but maybe I should."

"If you win, you can always give her the prize," Molly said.

"I *could*." Laura grinned slyly. "We're good friends and all, but fair is fair, right?"

The women ahead of them strolled away with their packets, so the Bakehouse Three stepped up to sign in. All three entered the charity raffle, which cost only five dollars per entry. Laura bought two, Molly noticed with amusement.

They had packets in hand, containing class agendas, a program, and other information, when Patsy Mae came running up. "There you are," she said, slightly breathless. "I just got down here." She put a hand on Laura's arm. "I had the most brilliant idea for my new book, and before I knew it, hours had passed. Good thing my room is right upstairs."

"The life of a writer," Laura said. "Inspiration comes first. But you missed all the excitement. The lights went out."

"I know," Patsy Mae said, rolling her eyes. "Fortunately my laptop was fully charged, or I would have lost everything." She glanced around the circle of faces. "Want to sit together?"

"Sure," Molly said. "But I've got to go perform first. See you back at the table." She spotted several other Yoopers, including Mayor Tavish Calhoun and police officer Greer Anderson, making their way to the ballroom entrance.

After stopping by the table to drop off her packet and retrieve her bagpipes, Molly hurried to join the rest of her troupe. Alastair raised a brow as she edged past him into the back room. "Good timing, Molly. We're about to go on."

"I know." Molly smiled a greeting at the other pipers as she hastily put her instrument together. Then she took a few deep breaths to prepare both mind and body. Bagpipes were a wind instrument, after all.

At their leader's instruction, they lined up in the hallway, moving to fill the gaps left by missing members. Fergus was last to arrive, understandably due to his resort commitments, and then they were ready to begin. Alastair gave the signal and they burst into "A Red, Red Rose," an ideal choice for a romance conference.

The evocative and keening notes of bagpipes playing in unison filled the ballroom as they entered. Even though she was playing, Molly felt a chill run down her spine. Nothing conjured Scotland better than performances on this traditional instrument. The Yoopers made a circuit, then stood at the front of the room. They played "For the Love of a Princess," then finished with "Scotland the Brave," a rollicking favorite.

As the Yoopers filed out again, Molly heard Mavis Baines, the event coordinator and leader of the Scottish Romance Authors Association, begin her welcoming speech. In their small staging room, the pipers quickly packed away their instruments, eager to rejoin the conference.

Even Mayor Calhoun was in a hurry. "Sandra's saving me a plate of goodies," he said. "I was late getting here from the office." Apparently his wife was a romance fan.

"I'm glad you made it," Molly said. "There was one song where I was definitely playing follow-the-leader."

The mayor shook his head. "You did fine, Molly. Better all the time."

"Thanks," Molly said, grateful for the encouragement from a more experienced piper. Her phone, which had been silenced and left in the room during the performance, buzzed with an incoming call from her daughter, Chloe.

Rather than let it go to voice mail, Molly found a chair and sat while the other Yoopers gradually drifted back to the ballroom. "Hey, Chloe," she answered. "How are you?"

Her daughter gave a happy sigh. "I had the best day." Chloe worked as a veterinarian in Milwaukee, and she often had amusing and heartwarming stories to share about her furry patients. Today, Chloe was wrapping up the saga of a stray cat who'd given birth to six kittens at the clinic. Five kittens had been adopted, and a kind client had taken the mother and the last kitten home.

"That's so sweet," Molly said. "I love your stories."

Chloe laughed. "And I can't wait to hear yours from the romance convention. Be sure to take some pictures of Gregory Gregg for me."

"I'll try," Molly said. "And on that note, I'd better get going. Carol and Laura are probably wondering where I am."

After disconnecting with a promise to check in later in the week, Molly tucked away her phone and picked up her bagpipes case. Since the room wasn't secure, she didn't want to leave the instrument there unattended.

Voices drifted down the hallway, growing louder as they drew closer. "Please don't do it," a woman said, pleading in her voice. "You're going to ruin everything."

"I'm sorry, but I have to," came the reply. This voice was male, deep and rich. "I don't have a choice."

Molly froze, uncertain what to do. It was too late to leave the room and pretend that she hadn't heard anything. She could shut the door, though. As she was moving in that direction, the woman spoke again.

"There's always a choice." She sounded almost frantic. "If you go ahead, then . . . we're *over*."

A pause followed her ultimatum. "I'm sorry you feel that way." The man sounded calm, almost resigned. "But I'm not changing my mind. I'll be in my room if anyone needs me."

The woman burst into tears—noisy, gulping, helpless cries that tore at Molly's heart. Acting almost on instinct, Molly ran out of the room toward her, hoping she could do something to help.

Alyssa Martin was standing in the middle of the hall, shoulders hunched as she sobbed into her hands. As Molly approached, she lifted her head, revealing a mascara-streaked, tearstained face. Her gaze was distant, her eyes blank with pain. "I can't believe it's over. Gregory was the love of my life. What am I going to do?"

Molly's answer was to murmur comfortingly as she put an arm around the younger woman. With the other hand, she foraged in her pocket for tissues. Finding a small packet, she handed them over.

Alyssa took the tissues and pulled one out, then blew her nose with a honk. "Gosh, you must think I'm a mess. Falling apart this way." She tried to laugh, but it fell flat.

"Not at all," Molly said briskly. "Happens to all of us, sooner or later."

The editor dabbed at her eyes with a clean tissue. "What? Making a fool out of yourself over a man?" She sniffed. "Is true love even possible nowadays?"

Molly sensed that was a rhetorical question and didn't venture to answer. But how ironic that an editor of romance novels had doubts about love in real life. Well, maybe that was why many loved the genre so much. Happily ever after was a requirement of the plot, unlike in real life.

"I don't have all the answers," Molly finally said. "Not even a few, some days. But I do know this. When it's right, nothing can keep you apart. And if it's wrong? Well, better to find out sooner than later."

Alyssa darted a glance at Molly's face, and what she saw must have convinced her, because she nodded. "Thanks. I'm sorry. I don't even know your name. But you look familiar."

Molly put out her hand. "I'm Molly Ferris. I own the bakehouse downtown. You were in there this morning."

Alyssa put a hand to her head then shook Molly's. "Oh, that's right. I couldn't place you at first. By the way, the scones were fabulous."

"I'm glad," Molly said. She hesitated, not sure what else to say, if anything.

But Alyssa gave her a graceful exit. "I'm going to nip up to my room for a bit and freshen up. Please don't let me keep you any longer." She gave Molly a quick hug. "Thanks for caring."

Molly watched the editor walk away, then returned to the room to pick up her bagpipes. She'd never been to a romance convention before, but so far there seemed to be as much drama in real life as on the page.

4

"When was the last time we ate somewhere else for breakfast?" Carol asked, taking a plate off the pile. The Bakehouse Three stood in the buffet line in the ballroom. Bridget and their other part-timer, Hamish Bruce, were covering the bakehouse, which meant a rare midweek day off.

"I don't remember," Molly said. "But it's a treat." She eyed a pile of plump breakfast sausages and speared two with the serving fork.

"Belgian waffle?" a cook asked, poised to pour batter into an iron.

Molly considered. She usually didn't eat a big breakfast, but maybe she could splurge. "Yes, please," she finally said.

Carol and Laura wanted waffles as well, so the server filled three irons. While the women waited, they gathered the rest of their breakfast items.

Then, carting full plates, they joined Patsy Mae at a table near the back where she'd been saving seats.

"Good morning," Patsy Mae said. "It's a lovely day, isn't it?"

Indeed, sunshine and blue skies greeted them outside the tall ballroom windows. Although thunderstorms had swept through the night before, the humidity and temperatures were swiftly rising again.

"Someone's in a good mood," Carol said with a smile. "Did you sleep well?" She picked up the coffee carafe set on the table and filled three mugs.

Patsy Mae stretched with a sigh. "Did I ever. This place has the most comfortable beds. I slept like a lamb." She picked up her fork and chased a chunk of sausage around her plate. "And the food is divine."

"I'll be sure to give your feedback to the owner," Molly said, pleased to hear this praise. She knew how hard Fergus and his son, Neil, worked to make their guests happy.

"So this morning is our herbal tea class," Carol said, checking her schedule in between bites. "Are you taking that one, Patsy Mae?"

Patsy Mae checked her own program. "I sure am." Her chin rose. "And after lunch I have a one-on-one with Caroline Callahan. I saw she had an empty slot, so I took it."

"Are you sure that's a good idea?" Molly asked, her heart sinking as she pictured the stout, sour-faced woman with blonde curls she'd encountered the evening before. "I thought you didn't trust her." What if Caroline passed along Patsy Mae's new idea to Madelaine?

"Oh, I'm not sharing my new book with her." Patsy Mae picked up the coffee carafe and splashed some into her cup. "I'm going to ask about the package I sent her last year." She lowered her voice. "The book Madelaine stole."

"That's brave of you," Carol said with admiration. "What do you think she'll do?"

"I have no idea," Patsy Mae said. "But I want to see her face when I bring it up." A wicked smile played around her lips. "Don't worry, I won't accuse her of anything. I'll just ask what she thought of my book. Pretend I'm looking for feedback."

Laura gave a low whistle. "Patsy Mae, you amaze me."

Their friend ran a hand through her hair, her expression rueful. "I guess at this age, I'm finally tired of backing down and playing it safe. If losing Bo taught me anything, it's that you have to grab life with both hands." She growled playfully as she half stood and pretended to grab thin air with both hands. "Squeeze every last drop out of it."

Perhaps Patsy Mae was a little too loud and emphatic, because the women at the next table stared, then nudged each other and whispered.

Patsy Mae sat down with a plop and laughed. "Sorry. I guess I'm a little worked up today. I want to move ahead in my career, and it's frustrating. I've had so many setbacks and dead ends."

"I can only imagine," Molly said with sympathy. She noticed Mavis Baines moving to the microphone at the front of the room. Gregory Gregg was with her, and another woman was holding a box decorated with construction paper hearts. Molly pointed. "They must be doing the dinner drawing."

Carol and Laura turned to watch, and Patsy Mae sat straighter in her chair. She held up both hands, fingers crossed, and squeezed her eyes shut. "Please, please, please," she murmured under her breath.

"Good morning, everyone," Mavis said, her voice booming over the system. The clatter and voices echoing in the room slowly ground to a halt. "I'm thrilled to let you know that it's time to pick a winner for our raffle. One lucky conference attendee will be dining with Gregory Gregg this evening at the lovely King's Heid Pub here at Castleglen." Cheers went up, along with a few cheeky whistles.

The other woman shook the heart-dotted box and held it out to Gregory. Moving slowly, with dramatic flair, he stretched out a hand and reached into the box.

"I promise I'm not cheating, ladies," he said. "I'd be happy to dine with any of you."

Anyone but Alyssa Martin, Molly guessed, spotting the editor standing near a window, about as far away from Gregory as she could get. From the frown on the young woman's face and her cross-armed stance, Molly guessed they hadn't made up.

After moving his hand around, the audible rustle captured on the microphone, Gregory withdrew a slip of paper. Without reading it, he held it out to Mavis. "Please read it for me," he said, one hand over his eyes. "I can't bear the excitement and suspense."

A woman nearby flapped her program like a fan. "Me neither, honey," she said to the laughter of her companions.

Lips pursed, Mavis squinted at the paper. She cleared her throat. Finally, the tension in the room at fever pitch, she announced, "And the winner of a dinner with Gregory Gregg is . . . Patsy Mae Wallace."

Patsy Mae jumped up with a shriek. She began clapping her hands and bouncing up and down. "I won! I won!"

The other attendees began to clap, slowly at first, then increasing in volume as Patsy Mae danced up front in response to Mavis's gesture. Mavis introduced her to the attendees and to Gregory, who bent over her hand in a courtly gesture. The crowd went wild over this, and Patsy Mae blushed bright red. She was almost tongue-tied as she gazed up at Gregory, obviously starstruck.

Molly was glad something had gone right for Patsy Mae. She deserved it.

After breakfast, the four women attended the vendor fair being held in a large adjacent room. Around forty booths were selling items themed to the conference, such as books, costumes, and trinkets.

Patsy Mae beelined to one of the largest booths, which offered costume rentals. "I'm going to rent a dress for tonight," she said. "And y'all need ball gowns for the dinner dance."

Molly glanced at her friends. "I hadn't thought about a ball gown. You don't think my Yooper costume will work?" Even as she said it, she realized that, while attractive, the traditional costume wasn't quite appropriate for a formal event.

"No way," Laura said briskly. She pulled a rustling rose silk from a rack and thrust it at Molly. "Try this on."

"It's beautiful," Molly admitted. The dress was a dream, with tucks and flounces and sprays of lace. She read the posted rental fees, which were very reasonable.

"Rent it quick," Carol said. "Before someone else snaps it up." She held a rich gold-colored velvet up to her body, a color that flattered her dark skin and salt-and-pepper hair. "I love this one."

"Good pick," Laura said. She was rifling through greens that would enhance her auburn hair. She squealed when she came upon a creamy celadon satin. "I don't usually go the princess route, but this is fabulous."

Patsy Mae was browsing another rack. "Look at this," she said, holding up a semiformal dress in black velvet. It was long but simple in style. "Think this will work for dinner?"

"It's perfect," Carol said, then lifted the hanger in her hand. "I'm going to try this on."

All the gowns were perfect fits, so they filled out rental forms and made arrangements to pick up the ball gowns the day of the event.

"These will all go in the back room," the attendant said. She was dressed in Scottish clothing that befitted a market stallholder in the 1700s. "We attach a copy of the contract to the garment's bag and put it on a private rack for safekeeping." She handed Molly her copy of the rental contract. "Bring this when you pick it up."

Before Molly left the booth, she snapped a photo of the rose gown and sent it to Chloe. She knew her daughter, who had loved pretending to be a princess when she was younger, would get a kick out of it. The reply came back almost immediately. *Gorgeous! Should I start calling you Your Majesty?*

"We'd better hustle," Carol said after all the transactions were complete. "Our class starts in five minutes."

The herbal tea class was held in a small meeting room overlooking a beautiful flower garden in full bloom. Lines of tables were set up facing the front, each place set with an array of tools and containers.

"Find a spot, ladies," Myra Loganach called out as they entered. Myra and her husband, Ewan, owned Loch Mallaig's Two Scots Guesthouse, known for its delightful tea and snacks.

Molly smiled a greeting at Myra, whose thin figure was draped in a flowing skirt and a white blouse covered with a tartan apron. A matching kerchief was tied over her short brown hair.

The four women found places next to each other at the back. There were two other spots at the table, with Hamish's wife, Joyce, already at one. The other, next to Molly, was empty.

The plump and sweet Joyce greeted them with enthusiasm. "I'm so glad you signed up for this class. I can't wait to try some new concoctions on Hamish."

The women laughed, thinking of their employee's somewhat cantankerous nature. If there was one thing certain about Hamish, it was that he had opinions.

The tables had almost filled up as attendees filtered into the room. At the last minute, Alyssa came striding in, talking on her cell phone. Seeing the empty space beside Molly, she headed over, still chatting.

Giving Molly a bare glance, Alyssa said into the phone, "He won't talk to me." A pause. "I know. It's awful." She listened for another moment then sighed. "Okay. I'll do my best."

Molly wasn't trying to listen, but it was unavoidable. She assumed Alyssa was talking about Gregory Gregg, though she supposed someone else could have been the topic of discussion.

Up at the front of the room, Myra clapped her hands for attention. "Are we ready to get started?" The chattering voices ceased as everyone focused on the teacher. Everyone but Alyssa, who was still on the phone.

Myra watched Alyssa, and soon so did everyone else. Finally the editor sensed that she was the center of attention—and not in a good way. "I have to go," she whispered hastily into her phone. "Talk later." She disconnected and put the phone face down on the table. "Sorry," she said to the room at large.

The instructor nodded, accepting her apology. "Today we're going to make three teas using flowers commonly grown in Scotland. In the days before prescription drugs became common, people relied on herbs to treat many common ailments."

Myra began describing the plants and their properties, instructing the students to examine and sniff the dried petals and buds at their stations.

"We're going to make elderflower tea," she said, "which is good for treating colds and other respiratory illnesses."

Joyce waved a hand. "I've heard about elderberry syrup," she said. "You can even buy it in the store now."

Myra nodded. "That's right. Elderberry is a very valuable plant. Elderflowers are what bloom before the berries are formed." She next talked about a Highland blend of heather, juniper, lemon balm, and rose hips, which was used to invigorate, and finally, a rosebud tea.

As the group admired the cluster of dried roses to be used in the tea, Alyssa called out, "Does it work for broken hearts?"

"Perhaps," came Myra's answer. "But the traditional use is for digestion and relaxation."

Molly sent Alyssa a sympathetic expression, but the other woman was focused on playing with the tea ingredients, moving them around her station. She had a feeling it would take more than a pleasant tea to help Alyssa forget her troubles.

After mixing the herbal concoctions, they brewed teas using electric kettles, then sipped small cups of each flavor. The remaining mixtures were theirs to keep, each stowed in a small muslin bag tied with ribbon.

"This was fun," Carol said as they wrapped up and tucked away their bags of tea. "Let's have lunch."

Molly realized she was hungry, which was surprising after her large breakfast. Then she checked the time and saw that their last meal had been hours earlier. "Sounds good. We have a little while before our letter-writing class."

Laura wanted to check in with Hamish, so Carol, Molly, Joyce, and Patsy Mae waited while she placed the call. The other students had left the class, leaving the friends alone in the room.

"What's going on with Alyssa Martin?" Patsy Mae asked. "Do you think she and Gregory are having romantic troubles?"

Molly winced at the question. She had no desire to betray Alyssa's confidences. Thankfully Carol spoke up. "Maybe you can find out tonight at dinner."

"Maybe so." Patsy Mae considered this. "Not that it's any of my business. But you have to admit it was strange that she mentioned being heartbroken."

"Alyssa didn't say that *she* had a broken heart," Carol pointed out. "She merely wondered if rosebud tea was good for one."

Thank goodness for Carol's logical mind. Molly exhaled, glad the topic had been avoided. She noticed that Laura had hung up. "Everything good at the bakehouse?"

Laura nodded. "They weren't terribly busy, and neither is the rest of downtown. Hamish thinks everyone is here."

"I think so too," Joyce said. "I've seen so many familiar faces today. This conference is quite a draw locally as well as from around the country."

The women wandered out into the hallway. Lunch was being served in the ballroom so they headed in that direction. Joyce spotted a women's restroom. "I'd like to pop in there and wash my hands before lunch."

"We all should," Carol said.

Most guests were already at lunch, so only one woman was in the bathroom, standing at the sink and applying lipstick. It was Caroline Callahan.

When Patsy Mae saw the agent, she took a step backward and almost trod on Molly's toe. Molly put a hand out to steady her friend. Then, apparently gathering her courage, Patsy Mae charged forward and approached Caroline.

"Hi, Ms. Callahan," she said in a bright and cheery voice. "I'm Patsy Mae Wallace. We have a meeting scheduled this afternoon to discuss my novel."

Caroline eyed Patsy Mae in the mirror, a disdainful expression on her face. Still staring, she ran water, rinsed her hands, and then noisily pulled out a paper towel. Crumpling it between her hands, she said, "Sorry to disappoint you, Ms. Wallace, but my one-on-ones are canceled this afternoon. We don't have a meeting." She tossed the ball of paper towel toward a bin, then swept past Patsy Mae and out the restroom door.

5

"Oh my, she's a rude one," Joyce blurted once the restroom door closed behind Caroline. "What was that all about?"

Patsy Mae shook her head. "I guess my appointment is canceled."

"That's too bad," Molly said. "But really, Patsy Mae, you don't want to work with Caroline anyway."

A trio of women burst through the restroom door and Molly stepped aside as they flocked toward the sinks.

"You're right," Patsy Mae said, a frown creasing her forehead. "But I sure hope she doesn't blackball me with other editors or agents."

Before Molly could ask if that was possible, a woman with gray curls and glasses glanced over at Patsy Mae. "I know who you are. You're the lucky duck who is having dinner with Gregory Gregg. Patsy Mae Wallace, right?"

The woman's companions surrounded Patsy Mae with cries of excitement. "What are you going to wear?" another inquired. Her cheeks pinking prettily, Patsy Mae told them about the dress she had reserved and said how excited she was to have the honor of dining with Gregory.

"I couldn't help but overhear what you were talking about," the first woman said. "Maybe Gregory Gregg can help you with your books. I know that's one reason I wanted to have dinner with him."

Her friends hooted. "That's what you say now, Linda," one teased.

"It's true," Linda said. "I was going to use it as research. Dinner with a handsome Highlander." She clasped her hands and sighed dramatically. "And he's got the ear of editors, I hear."

"You mean Alyssa Martin?" Patsy Mae couldn't control her mouth, which turned down in a sour expression.

"Oh, her of course." Linda pulled out a comb and ran it through her curls. "But there are others Gregory works for. Joe Byers, for example. He's an editor at Highland Hearts."

"I've heard of Joe," Patsy Mae said thoughtfully. "Maybe I should send my books to him."

"I would," Linda said. She tossed her head, making her curls dance. "He just gave me a three-book contract."

Her friends squealed. "It's so exciting!" one said. "Linda is going to be a published author."

Linda raised a rueful eyebrow. "Finally. After the longest five years of my life." Then she grinned. "Good luck to you, Patsy Mae."

"Thanks so much, Linda." Patsy Mae beamed, her spirits obviously lifted by the conversation. "You've given me hope."

As they left the restroom, Linda called, "That's the journey to becoming a published author in a nutshell. The triumph of hope over experience." The closing door cut off the sound of the women's laughter.

In the dining room, lunch was well underway. After dropping their bags at an empty table, Molly and her friends got into line, filling bowls with creamy tomato soup and selecting sandwich halves from platters. Side salads rounded out the selection.

Molly had decided on a roast beef sandwich with Havarti cheese when Fergus sidled up next to her. "How's everything going, Molly?" he asked. "Are you enjoying yourself?"

"I sure am," she told him. "This morning we made herbal tea and this afternoon we're going to write . . . letters by hand." She felt her face heat up. She'd almost said *love* letters, but somehow found herself unable to say that one word. The purpose of the class was more to help authors create authentic missives in their historical novels, but the Bakehouse Three thought it would be fun to try.

His eyes twinkled in a teasing manner. "I think I know the class you mean." He peered past her at the table of food. "I have a minute. Mind if I eat with you ladies?"

"Please do," Molly said, her heart warming. "It will give us a chance to catch up." Since moving to Loch Mallaig from Chicago, where she had been an event planner, Molly had gotten used to talking to Fergus almost daily. Not only was he a good listener, but she appreciated his sensible viewpoint.

Fergus went to the back of the line, which was short, and soon joined Molly and the others at the table. "How is Hamish doing?" he asked Joyce politely.

"He's great," Joyce said. "Thanks for asking." Then her eyes lit up. "Listen to this. He spotted a golden-winged warbler the other day. They're becoming quite uncommon, so he got to file a rare bird alert. He loves doing that."

"That's good news, then," Fergus said. "Tell him to keep up the good work."

Molly bit into the sandwich, enjoying the contrast of tender, spicy meat with crisp lettuce and creamy mayonnaise. "I take it you sorted out the electricity problem?"

Fergus, who had been eating his own sandwich, dabbed at his mouth with a napkin. "We did. A tree that was damaged in the storms a couple of nights ago finally came down." His expression was rueful. "Taking a pole with it. Then we had a glitch with the backup generator, as you know, since you were stranded in the dark. But all's well now."

"I'm glad to hear it," Molly said. She couldn't imagine how unpleasant the event would be without air-conditioning on a hot day like this. "Your handyman seemed to be on the ball."

"Reg is amazing. Can fix anything." Fergus forked up potato salad. "He came along at the perfect time too. My regular handyman broke his leg in a car accident a couple of weeks ago, and Reg arrived at the very moment when I was beginning to wonder what we would do."

"Wow, that's fortunate," Molly said. "Is he from the area?" Molly had never seen him before but she was a relative newcomer to the Upper Peninsula.

Fergus shook his head. "He moved from Detroit. He likes to fish, so he came up here to see if he could get work."

"Sounds like someone else I know." Molly smiled at Carol, whose husband, Harvey, was an avid fisherman. Laura had grown up nearby, and Molly and Carol had vacationed in the UP frequently while growing up, so the trio certainly understood the area's allure.

"Everyone enjoyed the baked goods yesterday," Fergus said, talking to all three. "We'd like to order mini scones for tomorrow's tea, if you have time."

"Since you're head baker, you should take this one," Carol said to Laura. "But let me know what I can do to help." Carol was second-in-command in the bakehouse kitchen, an excellent baker in her own right who specialized in creating gorgeous birthday and wedding cakes.

Laura thought for a moment. "We can do that." She pulled out a pen and pad of paper. "What were you thinking?"

Fergus named the flavors that they wanted to order and Laura wrote them down, along with quantities. "I really appreciate you doing this for us," he said.

"No problem." Laura's smile was genuine. "Every time we serve baked goods here, we get new customers at the shop. Not only do we appreciate the extra business, it helps build our reputation."

"A win-win, then," Fergus said lightly. "So are you ladies ready for the closing ball?"

"We sure are," Carol said. "We reserved gowns today. Now I've got to convince Harvey to reserve Scottish white-tie attire."

"I love the dress I picked," Molly said. She couldn't wait to wear the pretty rose gown. It was so much fun to get dressed up that she wondered why she didn't do it more often. Of course, nowadays people rarely wore formal or even semiformal outfits.

"Save a dance for me," Fergus said, smiling at Molly. "It should be great fun."

"Of course I will," Molly murmured, quickly turning her attention back to her lunch. She was sure Fergus would be in great demand at the ball since women at the conference far outnumbered the men. Maybe some locals from Loch Mallaig would attend and help boost those numbers.

After lunch, Patsy Mae went to find the organizers of the one-on-ones to see if she could get a meeting with Joe Byers, the Highland Hearts editor. The Bakehouse Three and Joyce went to the love letter-writing class.

"You know what I'm going to do?" Joyce confided as they strolled toward the meeting. "Write Hamish a love letter. I haven't done that for years. He'll get such a kick out of it."

"Really?" Molly clapped a hand over her mouth. "I'm sorry, it's just . . ." Just that she couldn't imagine the irascible Hamish on the receiving end of a sentimental missive.

"He's a big softie under all that bluster, you know," Joyce said. "You simply have to separate the wheat from the chaff."

"His bark is definitely worse than his bite," Molly agreed fondly.

The young lady teaching the class introduced herself as Darcy Allen, romance novelist.

"How nice to meet you," Carol said. "I really enjoy your books."

Darcy's pale cheeks flushed with pleasure. "I'm so glad." She scanned the audience. "How many here are also authors?"

The middle-aged woman who'd given Patsy Mae a pep talk in the restroom was among those raising hands. "Hi, I'm Linda. And I recently got a three-book deal." The other women in the room clapped and whistled.

After the other writers said a few words about themselves, Darcy got down to business, flicking on an overhead projector. "It's hard to imagine now, in this age of instant communication, but letter writing was once a highly valued art."

She displayed examples of handwritten love letters on the screen, describing how these documents had become precious keepsakes passed down through the centuries. She also read a few to the audience. Then, judging they were adequately inspired, she instructed them to compose letters with quill and ink on pieces of ivory parchment paper.

Molly pondered for a few moments before starting. Whom could she write to? Maybe she should make someone up, an imaginary Scottish gentleman, perhaps. Then she had an idea. She dipped the quill into the ink and put tip to page. *Dear Kevin*, she began. She would write a letter to her departed husband, telling him how much he was missed and how much she had loved him. Then she would seal it up with wax and put it away.

This inspiration led her to write quickly and well, she thought, and she felt an unexpected sense of closure as she signed her name. Of course no one would read it, except maybe Chloe someday. Molly set her quill down and sat back, noticing that most of the other students were still scratching away.

Linda and her friends were seated behind Molly, and she could easily hear what they were saying. "I'm going to use this letter in a book," Linda said. "My hero is writing to my heroine."

One of her friends cooed approval. "I can't wait to read it." The woman paused. "Promise me one thing, Linda—that fame won't turn you into a nasty shrew like Madelaine."

Molly's ears perked up. They must be talking about Madelaine Alt. On behalf of Patsy Mae, who believed Madelaine had stolen her book idea, she listened hard.

"Yes, that was pretty awful," Linda agreed. "I couldn't believe she would treat Gregory that way."

The third friend gave a grunt of agreement. "I kind of wish we could have heard more. I mean, who could get angry with someone like Gregory Gregg? He's the perfect man."

"No one's perfect," Linda said. "But he comes pretty close."

Molly's mind spun into gear. What had Madelaine and Gregory been discussing? She shelved this information to discuss with Patsy Mae later.

Once class was over, the Bakehouse Three went up to Patsy Mae's third-floor room to visit with her before her date. Carol knocked.

"I'm coming," Patsy Mae sang out. They heard the click of a dead bolt and Patsy Mae opened the door. "You'll never guess what happened," she said in a gloating voice.

"What?" Carol asked as they filed in. "Come on, don't leave us in suspense."

Patsy Mae clasped her hands together. "Joe Byers wants to see my book. He loved the premise and the sample pages."

"Oh, that's wonderful," Molly said, giving her old friend a hug. "I hope he snaps it right up."

"Me too," Patsy Mae said. "Can I get you three a cold drink?" She gestured toward the kitchenette area, where there was a refrigerator. "I've got soft drinks, iced tea, and water."

"None for me, thanks," Carol said. "I wanted to wish you well, and then I've got to get going. Harvey and I have dinner plans."

"I have to leave as well," Laura said. "I'm going to swing by the bakehouse and do some prep. Fergus gave us a big order for tomorrow."

Patsy Mae's face was forlorn when she fixed her gaze on Molly. "Do you have to leave too?"

Molly made a quick decision. "I'll stay for a little while. Laura, can you let Angus out when you go to the bakehouse? He can play in the backyard until I get home."

"You bet," Laura said. She swooped in to give Patsy Mae a hug. "Knock him dead tonight, my dear. And good work with Joe. You're on your way."

Patsy Mae laughed as she returned the hug. "Thank you, Laura. I'll give you a full rundown about dinner tomorrow, I promise." She embraced Carol next. "And say hello to your wonderful man. I can't wait to see him and hear about his fishing exploits."

Carol rolled her eyes. "I'm warning you, once he starts in, you'll get quite the earful."

"I don't mind," Patsy Mae said. "Bo used to fish too. I heard more tall tales than you can imagine." She saw Carol and Laura out, then shut the door behind them and started toward the refrigerator. "Iced tea, Molly? I'd offer hot, but the microwave isn't heating right."

"Iced tea sounds perfect," Molly said, settling into a chair at the table. She thought of the conversation she had overheard during class and wondered how to broach the topic.

Patsy Mae uncapped two bottles of iced tea and handed Molly one. Then she went over to the desk. "Hold on, I've got to call Gregory. He wanted me to touch base before our date." She picked up the housephone and dialed, then frowned. "He's not picking up. He said to call him at four, though."

"Maybe he's not in his room yet," Molly said. "Give him a few minutes."

"All right." Patsy Mae sat in the other chair with a sigh. "I hope he didn't decide to ditch me." She picked up her iced tea and took a long swallow.

"Why would he do that? It's for charity." Molly grinned. "Plus, you're a wonderful dinner date. He's getting the long end of the stick."

Patsy Mae shrugged, then changed the subject. "How was your letter-writing class?"

"It was great." Molly filled in her friend. Then, despite feeling like a gossip, she asked, "Remember Linda, the writer we met in the restroom?"

"The angel who referred me to Joe? How could I forget?"

"Apparently she overheard Madelaine Alt arguing with Gregory. I'm not sure if that's useful to you or not, but I wanted to mention it."

Patsy Mae rose from her chair, frowning in thought. "Why would she argue with her cover model? Maybe he wants to quit. That has to be it." She reached for the phone and dialed again. "Still not there. Or he's not answering."

"Why don't we go to his room and see?" Molly suggested. "If he's not there, you can leave a note."

Patsy Mae thought about this for a moment. "All right. What can it hurt?" She scrawled a note on the pad provided by the hotel and ripped the page off. "Let's go."

"Okay," Molly agreed, and followed Patsy Mae out to the hallway.

With most guests still attending the conference, the corridor was hushed and empty. Patsy Mae led the way. "He's on this same floor, but down at the end."

As they approached Gregory's room, Molly noticed that the door was ajar. Perhaps the room attendant was inside. Patsy Mae seemed almost afraid to knock, so Molly went ahead.

"Gregory?" Molly called. "Are you here?"

She pushed the door open a bit wider, revealing Gregory's massive, well-appointed suite. The room she was peeking into was a living room with a large tanning bed set up in the center. Lights indicated it was on, and since the lid was down, she guessed the male model was in there.

"Gregory?" she repeated.

No answer, but the bed was emitting an odd buzz. An unpleasant electrical smell hung in the air.

A chill went up Molly's spine. Something was terribly wrong, she just knew it.

6

"What's going on?" Patsy Mae pushed past Molly. "Is Gregory in there?" She made it partway into the room and stopped, cringing as though not wanting to intrude. "Is he still in that tanning bed?"

Molly grabbed her friend by the shoulder. "We need to get out of here. Something is wrong and we've got to call for help." She wrestled a reluctant Patsy Mae back into the hallway and shut the door.

"Are you sure?" Patsy Mae cast a fearful glance toward the suite. "What if we could help him? And that odor—I've smelled it before." No doubt she had, since her husband had been an electrician.

"I think we'd better wait for help," Molly said, patting her pockets. No cell phone. Then she remembered. It was in her tote, back in Patsy Mae's room.

The housephone. Molly trotted down the corridor toward where she'd seen one on the wall. It was closer than Patsy Mae's room.

Her friend tagged along, right on her heels. "What are you doing?"

"Using the housephone." Molly lifted the receiver off the hook and dialed the front desk. "I need Fergus MacGregor to come to the third floor. It's an emergency." She gave the room number. "And please call 911 for an ambulance."

Patsy Mae sagged against the wall. "911?" she repeated. "An ambulance?"

Molly guided her to a nearby chair. "Please sit. We don't need you fainting." Patsy Mae's face was dead white, and no wonder. Molly was running on adrenaline herself. But rather than sit, she paced back and forth, every fiber straining to hear the sound of help arriving.

Patsy Mae put a hand to her mouth. "This reminds me of Bo." Tears welled in her eyes and began to fall. Soon her shoulders were shaking with sobs.

Molly found tissues in her pocket and handed them over. *Please, please get here soon.* She stared at the elevator doors, willing them to open.

As if in answer to her silent pleading, the familiar hum of the elevator rising began, hopefully heralding Fergus's arrival. The ambulance had to come from town so it would take a few minutes more.

The elevator stopped and the doors opened, revealing Fergus. "What's going on, Molly?" he asked, his face creased with concern. He nodded at Patsy Mae. "Is she all right?"

"She's upset," Molly said in a low voice. "Her husband died a few years ago, and I think she's reliving it." She gestured. "But something is definitely wrong with Gregory Gregg. Come with me."

Leaving Patsy Mae still seated, Molly and Fergus hurried to Gregory's room. "The door is probably locked," Molly said. "It wasn't when we got here, but I closed it to keep people out."

Fergus swiped the lock with a master key and let himself in. Within thirty seconds, he emerged, his face gray with horror. "There is something definitely wrong," he murmured as he pulled out his phone. "You were right about that."

From what he said, Molly gathered he was checking in with the front desk. "Call 911 again," he said. "Tell them to send the police as well." The clerk's gasp was audible even to Molly, standing a few feet away. She said something inaudible before Fergus hung up.

Molly knew a call to the police meant one of two things—that someone had hurt Gregory or he was dead. Maybe both. "Is he . . . ?" She couldn't force herself to say the words.

"I'm sorry to report that he's gone," Fergus said, gnawing at his lower lip. "That's all I can tell you until help gets here."

She put up a hand. "I don't want to know the details." She glanced at Patsy Mae, who had stopped crying and was staring into space, sniffing. Molly really didn't look forward to giving Patsy Mae this terrible update.

The elevator doors opened again but instead of EMTs emerging, Alyssa, Madelaine, and Caroline got out. What were they doing here? Were their rooms on this floor? They spotted Patsy Mae and swooped down on her like birds of prey.

"What happened to Gregory?" Alyssa asked, practically shrieking. "I overheard an employee say they need an ambulance for his room." Caroline put an arm around the editor, trying unsuccessfully to comfort her as she burst into tears.

News certainly traveled fast, Molly reflected. It never ceased to amaze her.

"They shouldn't be here," Fergus murmured just loud enough for Molly to hear. Squaring his shoulders, he bustled toward the women. "Excuse me, ladies," he called in a firm, authoritative tone.

All four turned to watch the resort owner approach. Molly stayed where she was, well within earshot but safely out of the line of fire.

"I'm sorry to report that yes, there has been a fatal incident involving Mr. Gregg," Fergus said. "Authorities are on their way. I'm going to have to ask you to go to your rooms or downstairs. We need to clear the area." Fergus's phone rang. "Excuse me." He strode down the hall a short distance.

Madelaine held her ground, planting her legs wide. "What about you two?" She jabbed fingers at Patsy Mae and Molly. "Why are you still here?"

Caroline tugged at Madelaine's sleeve. "Maybe they're involved. They probably can't leave."

"Oh no, we're not *involved*." Patsy Mae jumped to her feet, fists clenched. "We came to check on Gregory when he didn't answer his phone. We were supposed to have dinner tonight."

"Huh," Madelaine said. "So you just *happened* to find him?"

Molly had heard enough. She marched toward the group. "Patsy Mae, don't say another word. You don't have to defend yourself to these women."

"You have to admit it's very odd," Madelaine said, not dropping the topic. "Gregory was a vibrant, healthy man. Until he was murdered."

"I can see why you're such a popular writer," Patsy Mae shot back. "You have a great mind for fiction."

Molly thought she might have to step between the two women but fortunately Fergus ended his phone call. His stern gaze acted like a splash of cold water on the warring women, who stepped apart with mutters.

"The team is on its way," Fergus said. He made shooing motions toward Madelaine, Caroline, and Alyssa. "Please clear the area."

"We can't until the elevator comes," Caroline pointed out, but the elevator had begun to whir and the doors opened shortly. Two EMTs pushed a gurney out, followed by Chief Owen Thomson—Alastair's son—and Officer Greer Anderson, a sharp-witted blonde Molly knew from The Piping Yoopers and considered a friend.

Fergus gave the EMTs the room number and they hurried away rolling the gurney. "Chief, thanks for getting here so quickly. Molly Ferris and Patsy Mae Wallace were first on the scene, but these other three ladies are leaving." He gave them a pointed stare.

Finally taking the hint, the trio entered the now-empty elevator, Caroline with her arm around a weeping Alyssa. The doors closed in front of them and they were gone.

"We'll be back," Chief Thomson said to Molly and Patsy Mae. "Wait here, please." The officers and Fergus hurried toward Gregory's suite.

Molly sat in a chair beside Patsy Mae. "How are you doing? Feeling any better?"

"I'm okay," Patsy Mae said with a sniff. "Oh, Molly, this is so awful. Poor Gregory. I can't believe he's dead. What a terrible loss." Tears began to fall again.

"It is," Molly said softly, tearing up herself. An untimely death was always tragic and this one was certainly sudden. Gregory was so well-known and beloved that she was sure the news would rock the romance world.

And poor Alyssa, who had lost the man she loved. They'd never have an opportunity to reconcile now.

Fergus was first to return, but he merely nodded at them as he strode past to the elevator. "I need maintenance records for a suite on the third floor," he said into his phone. He pressed the elevator button.

Molly wondered why Fergus needed maintenance records, what they were investigating.

Chief Thomson and Officer Anderson emerged from the suite, the chief giving Greer directives. "We're going to need the coroner and a crime scene team," he murmured, barely loud enough for Molly to hear. "And seal off the room."

As Greer made the calls, the chief continued toward Molly and Patsy Mae. "Is there a quiet place we can chat?" he asked. "This is a little too public."

"How about my room?" Patsy Mae offered. "It's right down the hall. I have a table and chairs where we can sit."

The chief nodded. "That will do for now." To Officer Anderson, he said, "Ask Fergus about a room we can headquarter in, will you? We're going to talk to Mrs. Ferris and Mrs. Wallace in Mrs. Wallace's room, but we'll need another spot."

Patsy Mae led the way to her room, Greer jogging to catch up after speaking to Fergus.

"Please excuse the mess," Patsy Mae said as they entered the hotel room. She gestured at the clothing laid out on the second bed. "I was planning to have dinner with Gregory Gregg, but then—" Her voice broke off with a sob.

"Why don't you tell us more about that?" Chief Thomson's voice was soothing. He waited for the women to sit before taking the remaining chair.

Patsy Mae waited a moment to compose herself. "I'm not sure if you're aware of this, but Gregory Gregg is . . . *was* the best-known male model in the Scottish romance world." She picked up a paperback from a stack and showed the officers the cover. "That's him. Anyway, there was a raffle here at the conference, and the winner got to have dinner with Gregory." She choked a little, patting her chest. "Sorry, my throat is dry." After taking a sip from her iced tea, which she'd left on the table, she continued. "I won, and the dinner was supposed to be tonight."

After letting Greer catch up with her notes, Molly added, "Gregory wasn't picking up when Patsy Mae called, as they had arranged, so we went down to the suite to see if he was there, and if not, to leave him a note."

"You still have the note?" Chief Thomson asked.

Patsy Mae foraged in her pocket and found the somewhat-crumpled piece of paper. She put it on the table, tried to smooth it, and handed it to Thomson. The chief looked it over, and then Officer Anderson put it into an evidence bag.

Molly sucked in a breath. They were obviously scrutinizing Patsy Mae in relation to Gregory's death.

"Did you speak to Mr. Gregg at all today?" the chief asked.

"Only once, after breakfast," Patsy Mae said. "That's when he told me to touch base before dinner. We were supposed to dine at King's Heid Pub tonight at seven. He said he had made a reservation."

Officer Anderson scribbled a note. "I'll confirm that."

"So you didn't visit Mr. Gregg's room at all today before you went down there with Ms. Ferris?" The chief's tone was steely, as if he were verifying a point.

Patsy Mae flushed red and she began to wave her hands around. "No I didn't. Honest. I was at the conference all day—well, except for when I took a walk this afternoon on the grounds to clear my head. It's gorgeous outside."

Molly almost said that she'd been with Patsy Mae since breakfast, but that wasn't exactly true. Patsy Mae hadn't gone to the letter-writing class with them. She'd had a meeting with Joe Byers, but beyond that, Molly had no idea where her friend had been.

"Why don't you tell us about your movements today?" Chief Thomson asked. "With approximate times, please."

Patsy Mae wrung her hands. "Why are you asking me all this? I didn't have anything to do with Gregory's death."

"It's just routine," the chief hurried to assure her. "I'm going to ask Molly the same questions."

He is? Molly began to think back over her day, trying to remember where she had been every moment. Of course, Carol and Laura could vouch for her. She'd been with them the whole time—except this afternoon, after they'd left for home.

Patsy Mae provided an account of her movements, with Molly confirming the times they were together. While Molly and the others were in the letter-writing class, Patsy Mae had taken a walk, trying to relax before her one-on-one with Joe Byers. After the meeting, she'd come back to her room to write, which had given her over an hour alone.

When it was Molly's turn, she gave a brief overview of her day. "After class, Carol, Laura, and I came up here to see Patsy Mae. She was excited about her dinner date with Gregory, and elated after her meeting with Joe. The other two had to go home, but I decided to stay for a while. And that's when we went down to Gregory's suite."

Her voice stuttered to a halt. The memory of the experience gave Molly chills. Would she ever forget the skin-crawling sensation she'd experienced when she peeked inside his room? Her every instinct had warned her that something was terribly wrong.

"When you're ready, Molly," the chief said, giving her a moment.

"I'm okay," Molly said. "I think something went wrong with the tanning bed. I smelled burned wiring."

The chief exchanged glances with Officer Anderson. "We can't comment on that," he said. "We haven't determined a cause of death yet."

"I smelled it too," Patsy Mae said. "My late husband was an electrician, and he always warned me about the signs of an electrical fire. When things overheat, they have a very distinct aroma."

"Did your husband teach you a lot about electricity?" Chief Thomson asked.

A prickle of warning crawled up Molly's spine, but before she could say anything, Patsy Mae smiled and nodded. "Oh, tons. He loved talking about his work. It was his passion. It was either learn to like it or be bored out of my mind." She laughed. "I even helped him on occasion. Never outside our house, of course. It wouldn't be legal anywhere else."

Molly saw to her dismay that Officer Anderson was dutifully jotting all this down. Patsy Mae had absolutely no motive to hurt Gregory Gregg, but she was informing the police that she might have the skill. And all that time alone when she claimed to be on a walk or writing in her room was the opportunity, unfortunately. The worst thing was, she had volunteered all this information without them asking.

Was jovial, kindhearted Patsy Mae unwittingly implicating herself as a cold-blooded murderer?

7

Someone rapped on Patsy Mae's door and Officer Anderson went to answer it. "Oliver is here," Greer told the chief after conferring with another officer, likely meaning local mortician and coroner Oliver Fitzgerald. "He wants to speak to you."

Chief Thomson rose. "I think we're done here for now," he said to Patsy Mae and Molly. "I may want to talk to you again, Mrs. Wallace. How long are you going to be in town?"

Patsy Mae appeared frightened. "I'm staying for the whole conference, so a few more days." She swallowed visibly, then asked, "Why do you want to talk to me again?"

"Just routine," the chief said. "In case we need to follow up on anything." He nodded goodbye to the women before hurrying to join Officer Anderson, who was still standing at the door.

As soon as the door closed behind them, Patsy Mae let out a wail. "Oh, Molly. I can't believe this is happening. Poor Gregory." She grabbed some tissues from a box on the table.

"I know," Molly said glumly. "It's awful."

"Why do you suppose they might want to talk to me again?" Patsy Mae asked. "Do they want to ask my opinion about how Gregory died? Something must have gone wrong with the tanning bed."

Molly studied her friend, who was clearly trying to help. "I'm sure they have experts they can consult. Please, Patsy Mae, don't offer any theories, okay? You don't want them to think—" Molly bit off the words.

But Patsy Mae caught on. "That I killed him?" Her eyes widened. "You don't really think that I'm a suspect, do you?"

Molly wasn't certain of anything. "We don't know enough to even guess. Maybe he died from a heart attack." At a knock on the room door, she got up. "I'll go see who it is."

"I don't feel like talking to anyone," Patsy Mae called after her. "I feel like curling up into a ball in my bed."

Quite understandable. Molly peered through the peephole. Fergus was standing in the hall. "It's Fergus. Can I let him in?"

"Oh, okay," Patsy Mae said. "He's all right."

Molly opened the door. "Hi, Fergus. Come on in." She stood back to let him enter the room.

"How are you two doing?" he asked after she shut the door. "It must have been quite a shock."

Patsy Mae barked a laugh. "You've got that right. And I feel awful. Thanks for asking."

Fergus glanced at Molly in inquiry. "I'm okay," she told him. "Iced tea?" She opened the refrigerator and pulled out a bottle. She and Patsy Mae still had some left.

"Thanks." He accepted the bottle and popped the cap. After he took a long swallow, he said, "I thought you might want an update."

"Of course we do," Molly said, taking a seat at the table and gesturing for him to join them. "Are you allowed to tell us anything?"

Fergus gave her a brief smile as he sat. "They're going to hold a press conference in my lobby soon. I think I can give you a preview."

"A press conference." Molly considered this. "Does the media already know?"

"Oh yeah," Fergus said. "The word went out on social media, and that's all it took."

Molly could imagine the news spreading like wildfire. Whenever a celebrity died, it was front-page news. And the handsome and well-known Gregory certainly fit the bill. No doubt he had fans coast-to-coast and even around the world.

"Oliver Fitzgerald is going to do an autopsy," Fergus said. "But he said that there was some kind of malfunction with the tanning bed."

"I knew it!" Patsy Mae cried. "We smelled the wires burning."

"It's terrible, but at least the room didn't catch on fire," Fergus said. "We fortunately have a state-of-the-art fire suppression system."

"Did the tanning bed belong to the resort?" Molly asked. She crossed her fingers that the answer was no, or else the resort might be found liable.

Fergus shook his head. "No, Gregory had it brought in. We had Reg hook it up and make sure it was working correctly. That's what's so strange about the situation."

"Reg the handyman?" Molly asked. "They must be questioning him then."

"They are," Fergus said. "He was up in the room earlier today replacing light bulbs, but he said all was well. Gregory wasn't using the bed at the time, though."

"So someone else went to the suite," Patsy Mae said. "Good. Maybe they'll stop questioning me."

"Patsy Mae is worried that she's a suspect," Molly said at Fergus's confused expression, then went over their conversation with the police.

"They don't even know if it's murder yet," Fergus pointed out. "Besides, Reg wasn't the only one who visited Gregory this afternoon. He saw Alyssa Martin headed that way after he left the suite. The police are also talking to her."

Molly took a breath, thinking of what she knew about Gregory and Alyssa. She was tempted to share the information with her friends but refrained. If she told anyone, it should be Chief Thomson. Not that she wanted to point a finger at the young editor, but the police needed to know the truth about Alyssa's relationship with the deceased man.

Fergus finished his iced tea. "I'd better get back to work. Please call if you need anything, Patsy Mae. And you too, Molly."

"Thanks, Fergus," Molly said. "We appreciate that. And the update." She got up to walk him to the door. "See you tomorrow."

He gave her a warm smile. "Have a good night. I'll touch base later."

Which meant an update when he knew more or that he was going to check in on her. She'd take either—or both. "Sounds good."

After she closed the door behind him, Patsy Mae said, "He's such a nice man. It's easy to tell that he cares a lot about you."

Molly's heart skipped a beat. "You think so? I care about him too. He's become a good friend since I moved to Loch Mallaig." She returned to her seat at the table. "We knew each other as teenagers, when I used to come here with my family."

"How lovely," Patsy Mae said. "Old friends are often the best friends." She sighed. "Nice as his place is, I'm not going to enjoy sleeping here tonight."

Molly could understand her concerns since Gregory's suite was right down the hall. "Why don't you come stay with me? It's not much, but it's comfortable. We can order food from the restaurant across the street."

Patsy Mae's face brightened. "I'd love to. I'm sure I'll feel better tomorrow."

Patsy Mae put together a small overnight bag, and they left the room a few minutes later. Molly was anxious to get home. Poor Angus must be missing her, although Bridget had let him out and so had Laura. She knew he'd be excited to meet Patsy Mae—and that the little dog's adorable antics might be just what the poor woman needed to forget some of her stress.

After an expectedly friendly greeting, Angus stayed with Patsy Mae while she got settled in Molly's den, which had a pullout couch bed for guests. Fondly reflecting on her dog's inherent knowledge of when someone needed a furry friend, Molly went to her tidy kitchenette and called Laura to give her the news about Gregory. Carol was already out to dinner with Harvey and she didn't want to interrupt their nice meal.

"I can't believe it," Laura said after a long, stunned moment. "Good thing you two went down to his room, or who knows how long he would have been lying there."

Molly hadn't thought of that angle, but Laura was right. Gregory could have lain undisturbed until morning if no one had come to his suite. Her phone beeped with another call. "Hold on, Laura. It's Fergus. I'm going to take it, but I'll be right back." She clicked over. "Hi, Fergus. I can't talk long, I'm on the phone with Laura."

"This will be quick," he said. "The coroner has ruled the death a homicide. Someone tampered with the tanning bed, and Gregory died of electrocution."

Molly gasped. Although she'd suspected something like this, it was still shocking to have it confirmed. It felt as if an ominous dark cloud moved overhead. "I'm so sorry to hear that. So it will be a full-blown murder investigation."

"I'm afraid so," Fergus said. "I asked if we ought to cancel the conference, but the police said we should continue. They don't want anyone to leave yet."

"I understand." Molly heard Patsy Mae humming in the other room. "By the way, Patsy Mae came home with me, if they need her for anything. No offense, but she wanted a change of scenery."

"Can't say I blame her," Fergus said. Voices and noise erupted nearby. "I'd better go. We have to deal with the press. They've gotten wind of the news."

"Good night, then." Molly switched back to Laura. "It's murder," she said. "Electrocution by tanning bed."

Laura whistled. "Wow, that is *terrible*. The poor man. What else did Fergus say?"

Molly shared the rest, including that the conference was still going on despite Gregory's death. They discussed arrangements for the next day, then Laura hung up.

Patsy Mae was singing. Molly sat on a chair, wondering what to tell her. She hated to wreck her friend's peace of mind. Angus, who had trotted into the room to check on her, studied her, head cocked, as if wondering the answer as well.

"How about this, Angus?" Molly fondled his silky ears. "We'll let Patsy Mae have a nice night. Time enough to dive back into the situation tomorrow."

Patsy Mae and Molly ended up having a very lovely evening indeed. They got to-go orders of Scottish food from Neeps and Tatties, which they ate at a patio table in the backyard. While they dined on meat pies and buttered turnips, Angus frolicked about, chasing squirrels and birds and his shadow.

"Loch Mallaig is wonderful," Patsy Mae said, breathing deeply. "The air is so fresh and fragrant."

"It's a beautiful time of year here, that's for sure." Molly smiled. "You might not have liked it a few months ago, in the heart of winter."

"I just might," Patsy Mae said, dipping her fork into her turnips. "Snow is so pretty. And we never get any in Louisiana. Once in a blue moon, maybe. But it melts right away."

"You're welcome back anytime," Molly said. "I'm so glad we reconnected."

"Me too," Patsy Mae agreed.

They spent the rest of the meal lost in nostalgia over mutual friends and college high jinks. After clearing up the remains of dinner, they took Angus for a walk in Dumfries Park. The lake was still, barely rippling in a very light breeze. The sun was quickly lowering, a fiery orb descending over the hills and reflecting in the water.

On such a warm evening, other people were in the park, playing Frisbee, jogging, or seated at picnic tables eating a meal. Angus greeted the dogs that came their way, some of them familiar friends.

Molly said hello to people she knew but didn't linger to chat. She was sure the news about Gregory had spread all through town. No good would come of talking about it in front of Patsy Mae, who appeared to have regained her equilibrium. Tomorrow was time enough to deal with the aftermath.

Laura arrived even earlier than normal the next morning, planning to dive right into the baking for Castleglen. Molly heard Laura drive in, and after feeding Angus and letting him out, she left Patsy Mae still sleeping and went down to join her friend in the bakehouse kitchen.

"Good morning," Laura said as Molly entered the room. She had already pulled ingredients out onto the counter and was measuring flour. "Sleep okay?"

"I did," Molly said, then surprised herself with a huge yawn. She grabbed a mug and poured a cup of coffee. "We took a long walk in the park, which was incredibly relaxing. But early this morning, my eyes popped right open." She added milk to the mug. "I sure hope they solve Gregory's murder quickly."

"Me too." Laura ran her finger down a recipe. "It's horrible."

The back door opened. A moment later, Carol bustled into the kitchen, shrugging out of her light jacket. "What's this I hear about a murder at Castleglen?"

Molly winced. "I'm sorry I didn't call you last night, Carol. I didn't want to ruin your date with Harvey."

Carol hung up the coat. "Thanks for that. We had a wonderful time. But it's all over the news this morning. Even the national news." She peeked into a mirror and ran a comb through her salt-and-pepper hair, then went to wash her hands.

"Fergus told me the media was already all over it," Molly said. She took a deep breath. "Patsy Mae and I were the ones who found him."

"What?" Carol whirled around, water droplets flying off her fingers. She reached for a towel to dry her hands, then rushed over and enveloped Molly in a warm hug. "You poor dears. Are you all right?"

Molly filled Carol in while pouring her a mug of coffee. After she handed it to her, she pointed upward. "Patsy Mae is upstairs. She didn't want to be alone last night."

"Who could blame her?" Carol took a big sip of coffee. "And here I was thinking about the nice time she must have had with Gregory on their date."

"I know. The date didn't even happen." Molly sighed, then set her coffee mug down and addressed Laura. "What can I do to help this morning?"

Laura gave orders and the three swung into action. Some of the baked goods were destined for the front cases, while others went into boxes for the resort. As they worked together, efficient with much practice, they hashed and rehashed the entire situation.

"Someone had it out for Gregory," Carol said. "But who? And why?"

"It might be related to what he and Alyssa were talking about," Molly said. She had set aside her qualms about sharing the overheard conversation, which she planned to mention to Chief Thomson. "He was going to do something and she didn't want him to. In fact, she broke up with him over it."

"What could it be?" Carol mused. "Maybe he was going to quit modeling?"

Laura shook her head. "Why would someone kill him over that? There are plenty of other models in the world." A teasing expression flashed in her eyes. "Like the men attending the conference."

"The repairman, Reg, told the police that he saw Alyssa visiting Gregory yesterday afternoon," Molly said. "He spotted her when he was leaving after fixing something in Gregory's suite."

"So there you go," Carol said, sounding satisfied. "She got revenge on him for her broken heart. She wanted him back and he said no."

Molly dug around in the pantry for a fresh bag of raisins. "I hate to think that, but it's better than them blaming Patsy Mae."

Carol lowered her voice. "Do you really think she's a suspect?"

"Looks like they do." To their shock, Patsy Mae had answered the question. Standing in the kitchen doorway, still dressed in her summer pajamas with her usually neat bob in disarray, she held out her phone. "Chief Thomson wants me to come down to the station." Her smile was crooked. "I need coffee. And an attorney."

8

After other cases involving friends, Molly practically had the number of a defense attorney on speed dial. "Here's Donal McNab's number," she said to Patsy Mae as she texted her his information. "Call him. He's the best around here."

"The Bulldog?" Patsy Mae laughed as she read the nickname that had come along with the contact info. "I'm not sure I want to know why you're acquainted with a defense attorney."

Molly gave a wry grin. "Trust me, the name fits. He's a good person to know."

"I'm going back upstairs to call," Patsy Mae said, heading for the door. "I'll keep you posted."

"I hope Donal is available," Carol said. "He's the best."

Laura deftly cut scones from a sheet of dough. "I'm sure that if he isn't, he'll refer her to someone good. He won't leave her hanging."

Molly took the cut scones and arranged them on a baking tray. "I hope this doesn't go beyond questioning. It's absurd to think that Patsy Mae killed Gregory. If only she hadn't mentioned that she knows a lot about electricity."

"Surely a guilty person wouldn't do that," Carol said. A timer rang and she peeked into the oven. "I hope they take that into account."

"I guess it's really a case of wrong place, wrong time," Molly said. "She was up in her room alone yesterday afternoon, so she *could* have gone to the suite."

"How would she have gotten inside?" Carol asked. "It's not like she'd tell Gregory to mind his own business while she tampered with his tanning bed."

Laura began to measure ingredients for a new batch of scones. "At least one mystery is solved." At their curious glances, she added, "The mystery of Gregory's tan. That man was always bronzed, no matter the time of year."

Carol snorted. "I've heard that tanning beds aren't good for you."

"You can say that again," Laura said drily.

Molly realized something. Whoever killed Gregory knew that he regularly used his tanning bed. Of course, most people didn't bring one along to a hotel, which indicated his commitment to a tanned glow went above and beyond the usual. But he could just as easily have not used it. Had he told someone he was going to be tanning? Or did he do it every day? A person less familiar with his routine, like Patsy Mae, might have failed at the murder attempt if Gregory decided he wasn't going to tan while at Castleglen.

Footsteps sounded on the stairs. Patsy Mae was wearing shoes this time. She burst into the kitchen, carrying her overnight bag and purse. "Mr. McNab is wonderful. He's coming right over to pick me up and drive me to the police station."

"That's great," Molly said, relieved that they now had Mr. McNab on the case. "Are you going to need a ride to the resort after?"

Patsy Mae shook her head. "No, he's going to drop me off. I'll meet you there." She gazed at the coffee maker. "He did request a large coffee to go and a scone, if you have an extra."

"Anything for someone who'll help you get out of this mess," Carol said. "I'll make up a to-go bag for you both." She grabbed paper cups and filled them with steaming hot coffee.

Since she was between tasks at the moment, Molly decided to slip upstairs to the office and call Chief Thomson. It was time to tell him about the conversation she'd overheard between Alyssa and Gregory. Maybe it had no bearing at all on the case, but he was the one who needed to determine that. She got the chief's voice mail, so she gave him a succinct summary, then gave him her cell number in case he wanted more details, even though she knew he already had it. There. Her duty was done.

When she returned to the kitchen, Patsy Mae was already waiting in the café area for Donal to arrive. It was time to open, so Molly unlocked the door to let waiting customers come inside.

One older man was carrying several folded newspapers under his arm. "Did you hear about the murder at Castleglen?" he asked another man who appeared to be about the same age.

"No." The man appeared aghast. "What happened?"

As the two got into line at the counter, the first man said, "One of those famous male models died." He lowered his voice. "In his tanning bed."

"Tanning bed?" the second man squawked. "You wouldn't catch me dead in one of those."

Customers nearby caught this unfortunate comment, and there was a brief, fraught silence before the chatter started up again. Donal McNab had pulled up in his luxury SUV and Patsy Mae bolted from the bakehouse, somehow managing to juggle her bags and the to-go order.

Molly, who was waiting on people, sighed deeply. They'd been open five minutes and already Gregory Gregg's death was the only topic on everyone's lips. There was absolutely no doubt it would be the same at the conference.

Once Hamish and Bridget arrived to take over, the Bakehouse Three headed out to the resort. Patsy Mae had sent a text saying that she was finished at the police station so would meet them in the ballroom, where presentations were being held during a breakfast buffet.

"I hope there's something left to eat," Carol said as they entered the resort lobby.

Standing at the front desk, Fergus overheard. "They're keeping the pans filled, so you're all set," he said with a smile. He turned to Laura. "Did you happen to bring our order for this afternoon?"

"We sure did." Laura pointed to the LaSalle, parked near the doors. "Once I get a cart, we'll unload and take everything to the kitchen."

"Perfect." Fergus hesitated. "There is one more thing." Once he had their full attention, he said with a wince, "I really hate to ask you this, but we're short of servers for the tea."

Carol put up a hand. "Say no more. We'll do it. But we'll have to nip home and get outfits if you want costumes."

"That would be wonderful," Fergus said. He waved a hand at his kilt. "As you can see, the staff is dressing up today. Something to do with honoring Gregory."

Molly gestured down at her slacks and blouse. "I guess we didn't get that memo."

Fergus offered to unload the LaSalle and park it for them, so the three women went along to the ballroom. With everyone already seated, the hallway was dead quiet. As they drew closer, Molly could hear the conference organizer speaking over a microphone. "This morning I have the pleasure and thrill of welcoming the foremost author in Scottish historical romance today, the author of dozens of best-selling novels, with millions in print worldwide, Madelaine Alt."

Under the cover of applause, the three slipped into the ballroom. A table near the buffet still had vacant seats, so they scurried along the carpet and sat down.

"Good morning, everyone," Madelaine said. Her voice was a little scratchy, and she cleared her throat. "I have a lot to share with you today. But first, I have a request. I'd like for us to honor Gregory with a moment of silence."

A wave of whispers went through the gathering, quickly silenced by Madelaine's stern stare as she gazed around the room. She cleared her throat again and bowed her head, hands folded. The attendees swiftly followed suit, as did the servers behind the buffet table.

The door to the hallway burst open, revealing Patsy Mae. Quickly realizing what was going on, she gave an apologetic shrug and tiptoed across the carpet. She slid into the empty chair beside Molly and bowed her head.

Madelaine lifted her head, signaling that the tribute was over, and a rustling noise filled the room as people shifted in their seats. One or two got up and headed for the coffee and tea table. Carol elbowed Molly. "I'm going up to grab some food. Coming?"

Molly nodded, sliding back her chair and rising. She and her friends pulled plates off a stack and moved along the food line as Madelaine began to speak.

"We'll be doing a more formal tribute to Gregory on the last night of the conference," the author announced. "But I'd like to show you a little of what we've put together now." The lights dimmed and she picked up a clicker. Pictures of the famous model began to flash on the large projection screen.

During this display, which showed a combination of candid photographs and book covers, the women filled plates and poured mugs of coffee. They arrived back at their seats as the last photo faded and the audience began to clap.

"Dear, dear Gregory," Madelaine said in a sad voice once the ovation died down. "We will always miss you." She clicked the device again and this time the cover of her latest book appeared. In a much brisker voice, she said, "I first got the writing bug back in . . ."

Madelaine's tale was compelling, a story of perseverance and hard work as she penned novel after novel, seeking an agent and then a publishing deal. Caroline Callahan had plucked her "from the slush pile," and the rest was history. Patsy Mae listened with rapt attention, even taking notes.

After Madelaine finished speaking, the crowd got up and started to move around. Some left for smaller sessions while others made their way to the replenished buffet and drink tables, Madelaine among them.

Seeing that the author had finished speaking to a pair of fans, Patsy Mae got up. "I need a refill. And I want to talk to Madelaine. Anyone coming with?"

Molly eyed her empty mug. "I'll go." For once the author was by herself, and she had something she wanted to ask. Doubt sloshed in her stomach along with her delicious breakfast, but she moved forward anyway.

Madelaine was adding cream to her coffee when the pair arrived at the station. "Hello," the author said, her tone distinctly frosty.

Patsy Mae appeared taken aback for a moment, then she plunged ahead. "What a wonderful talk, Madelaine. Your story is so inspiring."

"I'm glad you thought so." Madelaine finished stirring and tossed the tiny stick into the trash. She picked up her cup. "Now if you'll excuse—"

"Wait, please," Molly said, trying to inject warmth into her voice so as not to scare Madelaine off. "I have a question."

Madelaine peered at Molly down her long nose. "Yes? What is it?"

Molly glanced over her shoulder to be sure no one else was listening in. "Why did you jump to the conclusion that Gregory was murdered yesterday? None of us knew the cause of death yet, not even the police."

The author stepped backward, almost bumping the table. "Why…why, I don't know. I just thought . . . he was in good health. Perfect, in fact." She took a sip of coffee, her eyelashes fluttering. They were false, Molly noticed.

"There must have been something," Molly insisted. "Had he been threatened?"

Madelaine's hand fluttered, landing on her bead necklace, which she twisted. "Not to my knowledge, but he had enemies. Perhaps even a few deranged fans. Anyone with even a modicum of fame is hated by someone. In Gregory's case, perhaps that hate is what got him killed."

9

After delivering that unsettling remark, Madelaine murmured, "Excuse me, please," and stalked away.

"Wow," Patsy Mae said, fanning herself with her program. "That was a little scary."

"It sure was," Molly agreed, her mind whirring. Was Madelaine right in her assertion that Gregory had enemies? Obviously he had one at least—the person who'd killed him. But she'd thought maybe that was more personal, not related to his career as a model. Granted, celebrities of all stripes had been killed by fans.

Another thought struck Molly. Was Madelaine implying once again that Patsy Mae might be guilty? Patsy Mae had barely met Gregory, but she hadn't been shy about being somewhat starstruck. The woman certainly wasn't dangerous, though, no matter what Madelaine might be implying.

As she pulled the lever to fill her mug, Molly decided to tell Chief Thomson about this conversation as well as the other one she'd overheard. Maybe he could question Madelaine more forcefully and extract something useful, perhaps something she wasn't aware might be a clue. She and Gregory had worked together closely, after all.

Back at the table, Molly gave Carol and Laura the update. "I wondered what you were talking about," Carol said. "I could tell from here that Madelaine didn't like it."

Molly shrugged. It had been uncomfortable confronting the author, but on reflection, she didn't care. "She's the one who made the accusation. I couldn't let something like that go unchallenged."

Especially when the Bakehouse Three's friend was on the police's radar as a suspect.

"Go Molly." Laura lifted her mug in salute. "Madelaine will be a little more careful in the future."

"Are you signed up for Highland Dancing?" Patsy Mae asked, changing the subject. "I am."

"We are," Carol said. She nudged Molly. "Even Molly, who doesn't care much for dancing."

"That's because I have two left feet on a good day," Molly said. "But it will be fun." She pointed a finger at her friends. "Promise not to laugh when I mess up." Besides, she needed to practice for the ball. Fergus wanted to dance with her, so she had that motivation to improve.

"I can promise no such thing," Carol said solemnly, but her eyes twinkled when Molly glared at her.

"After class, I'm going back to the bakehouse for a while," Laura said. "Want me to pick up an outfit for you, Molly?"

"Sure, unless you need me this afternoon," Molly said. She'd planned on being at the conference, but the business came first.

Laura shook her head. "I'm going to work on my orders and do some prep for tomorrow's baking. Hamish and Bridget are holding down the fort just fine."

Molly told Laura where to find the clothing and shoes she wanted to wear to serve tea. "Thank you so much."

"What are friends for?" Laura asked. "Do you need anything, Carol?"

"Harvey is bringing my clothes," Carol said. "And I got him to agree to stay for tea." She chuckled. "He was a little leery about attending a romance conference."

"I don't blame him," Molly said. "Although he might be mistaken for a male model, especially if he wears a kilt."

Carol snorted with laughter. "Maybe if there's a Scottish retiree romance genre I don't know about."

"Harvey's gorgeous," Laura said. "Inside and out. We all should be so lucky to have a gem like him in our lives."

"Agreed," Molly said. Her friends' enduring and happy marriage was an inspiration to her.

Patsy Mae chimed in with agreement, then sighed. "I was a lucky one too. Bo was an absolute darling." She briefly seemed sad but then smiled. "At least when I write my love stories, I have real life to draw upon. I get to relive some pretty great moments with my Bo."

"Yes, there's nothing quite like falling in love," Carol said. "It's a wonderful experience."

Molly checked her phone, noticing the time. "We'd better finish our coffee, ladies. Our dance class is about to begin."

Two hours under the tutelage of a very patient instructor and the class was over. Laura headed for the bakehouse while Carol, Patsy Mae, and Molly went to the ballroom for lunch. From the vats and platters, Molly guessed they were having a soup and salad buffet for this meal. Tempting aromas of fish chowder and fresh rolls teased her nostrils as they entered the room.

A table right inside the doorway held schedules and sign-up sheets. Molly was signed up for Highland Hairstyles, but she decided to see what else was open in case she wanted to change. Her gaze fell on a sign-up sheet for sessions with Alyssa Martin.

"Patsy Mae, check this out," Molly said. When Patsy Mae edged up to the table, she pointed to an empty slot right after lunch. "Why don't you take this meeting with Alyssa?"

Patsy Mae hesitated. "I don't think she wants to talk to me. Not after the way she's been all cold toward me."

Molly put the pen in her friend's hand. "That's exactly why you should meet with her. There's something shifty about your book and Madelaine's, and you need to get to the bottom of it. I'll go with you, if you want," she added to clinch the deal.

"Me too," Carol said. Then she amended her offer. "No, I'd better not. Three will definitely scare her off. I'll go to the hairstyles class and get some good ideas for the ball."

Patsy Mae took the pen. "All right, I'll do it." She scrawled her name in the slot, so messily that it was hard to decipher. "She won't know it's me until I walk in."

After a delicious lunch, Carol went off to the class, and Patsy Mae and Molly prepared to meet with Alyssa. "Where is the meeting?" Patsy Mae asked. "Did you notice?"

"I didn't," Molly admitted. While Patsy Mae leafed through her tote for materials to show Alyssa, she went up to the table again. There it was, a side room she remembered near the room where she and the Yoopers convened before performances here.

Patsy Mae joined her, a cardboard portfolio in hand. "Oh, Caroline Callahan has room for a meeting after tea. Should I?" Then she giggled as she grabbed a pen. "Why not? I want to hear what she has to say about Madelaine's copycat book."

After Patsy Mae scrawled her name in the open slot, they headed off to the meeting with Alyssa. When they reached the room, they saw the door was slightly ajar. The voices of two women drifted through the crack.

"She's with someone," Patsy Mae whispered.

They paced about the corridor outside the room, waiting for the previous meeting to end. Finally the voices got louder as Alyssa and her guest approached the door. When it opened wide, Molly recognized Linda, who had recommended Patsy Mae approach Joe Byers.

"Hi there," Linda boomed when she saw them. "How'd it go with Joe?"

Patsy Mae glanced at a stone-faced Alyssa before pasting on a big smile. "It went great. He's very interested in my book."

Linda patted her on the shoulder. "Told you. Good luck." Linda said goodbye to Alyssa, then sashayed down the hall.

"Are you my next appointment?" Alyssa asked in a monotone. The young woman looked awful, her long hair limp and almost greasy. She wore no makeup, so the dark bags under her eyes stood out starkly against the pale skin of her face. Quite a contrast to the beauty who had first appeared at the conference on Gregory's arm. Sympathy twanged Molly's heart.

"I am," Patsy Mae said, her bold tone defying Alyssa to turn her away. She stared at the editor until the woman gave way, standing back to let them in.

Two chairs faced each other near the window, and Molly grabbed a third and placed it beside Patsy Mae. Alyssa sat down, hands folded in her lap, and Patsy Mae settled in her chair with much rustling of papers.

"What do you have for me?" Alyssa asked. "As always, we're seeking well-written historical romance set in Scotland. But we are especially interested in something fresh that breaks new ground."

Patsy Mae's eyes hardened. "Like a story set in the time of Queen Margaret?"

"Why yes," Alyssa said, her tone still calm. But a tide of red crept up her neck. "That's a very interesting era."

"I'll say." Patsy Mae gave a hooting laugh. "You published a book by Madelaine set in that time." She paused. "After I shared my idea and research with you. And Madelaine's agent."

Patsy Mae's tone was carefully neutral, not accusatory, but Alyssa flung herself back in her chair, eyes wide. "I don't remember that, but it often happens. People get similar ideas all the time. Why, I've seen similar books from different publishers come out the same week."

Patsy Mae leaned forward. "My book was based on my own ancestor, who was a very obscure woman. So forgive me if I don't believe it was a coincidence."

Alyssa shrank back so far Molly was afraid her chair would topple over. The red staining her skin had risen into her pale cheeks. "I wouldn't do that. I wouldn't steal someone's idea . . ."

Molly had no idea if that was true, although she fervently hoped so for the sake of all the hopeful authors who approached this editor. She decided to step in and ask a question on her mind before Alyssa blew up and ordered them out. "Alyssa, Madelaine has been saying some very interesting things lately. But not about a book."

That caught the editor's ear. "Like what?" she asked.

"You were there the first time," Molly said. "In the hallway outside Gregory's suite. Madelaine immediately jumped to the conclusion that Gregory was murdered. And today she told us that Gregory had enemies. Any idea what or who she was talking about?"

Alyssa gnawed at her bottom lip, then shook her head. "No," she said, her voice a squeak. "I have no idea." She jumped up from her chair, sending it rocking, then grabbed her bag. "Excuse me," she breathed before bolting for the door.

After it slammed behind her, Patsy Mae laughed. "I guess we got a rise out of her."

"I'll say," Molly replied. "I hope you don't mind me changing the subject. Her reaction makes me think she knows something about Gregory." She realized she hadn't told Patsy Mae about Alyssa's conversation with Gregory. "Something was going on between her and Gregory, bad enough that she broke up with him."

Patsy Mae's mouth dropped. "And you think it has something to do with his death? She went to see him that afternoon, right?"

"It might be related. It's certainly interesting." Molly leveled a serious gaze at her friend. "But let's keep this to ourselves, okay? If you weren't in the crosshairs yourself, I wouldn't have mentioned it. Gossip can be damaging."

Patsy Mae groaned. "Tell me about it. So many people are giving me strange looks today. They've obviously heard about the police questioning me." She inhaled deeply and sat up straight. "But I'm not going to let it get to me. I'm innocent, and I'm certain your wonderful Chief Thomson will prove that soon."

Molly sure hoped so. The lack of an arrest showed her that they didn't have enough evidence pointing to one suspect. *Yet*. Lacking evidence, they needed a confession or another move by the killer to bring the truth to light.

"Are you ready?" Molly asked, rising to her feet. There wasn't much point in hanging around in here. She doubted Alyssa would return. She glanced out the tall French doors leading to a patio. "Want to take a walk? We have time before tea."

The day was another warm one, so Molly and Patsy Mae stayed in the shade as much as possible. They wandered down to cliffs overlooking the loch, where a breeze gently blew off the water. Fishing boats, kayaks, and canoes dotted the blue water. By the time they returned to the resort's main building, Molly felt refreshed and renewed, if a trifle sticky.

"There you are." Laura met them in the main lobby. Already changed into her serving clothes, she was holding a garment bag with Molly's outfit.

"Thank you so much," Molly said. "How is Angus holding up?"

"He's fine," Laura said. "Now that the bakehouse is closed, Bridget is taking him for a walk in the park."

"She's so wonderful," Molly said. She paused to send Bridget a quick thank-you text. Their employee wrote right back, using emojis to convey that Angus was happily chasing squirrels. Molly put her phone away with a smile. "Well, I'd better go get ready. It's almost teatime."

For this afternoon's tea, the pastries and teapots were put on carts that the Bakehouse Three and a couple of other servers wheeled around the ballroom. As for all the events, most of the guests were dressed in costumes ranging from simple tartan skirts like Laura's and Molly's to fancy gowns. The staff also wore Scottish garb, and when Molly saw one man in a kilt kneeling on the floor near the buffet tables, she thought it was one of the male models.

But when he pushed to his feet, she saw it was Reg, the handyman. He wasn't bad-looking, but certainly not handsome enough to model, as Carol had pointed out. His nose was too big, his jaw too jutting, his eyes too small to be photogenic.

Molly caught his eye. "Is something wrong?"

"Not anymore," he said. "One of the outlets wasn't working, but it was a simple fix." His tool belt clanked as he slid a screwdriver into a pocket.

"Another problem?" Molly asked. "The resort sure has had a lot of them lately."

Reg shrugged. "Big place, lots of things to go wrong." He cracked a smile that lifted his features from ordinary to attractive. "Keeps me busy—and employed."

"That's good," Molly said. "The problem with Gregory's tanning bed wasn't the electrical system, was it?" She had heard it was sabotage but wanted Reg's take on the situation.

His brows rose into arcs. "No, ma'am. That wasn't to do with the house system. Something was wrong with the bed itself."

Molly shifted her weight, trying to appear casual. "Do you fix broken equipment too?" she asked impulsively. "Like in the gym? Or the kitchen?" It was doubtful he would tell her if he'd done something to the tanning bed, but she wondered if he *could*, if he had the skill. Some people were suggesting that Patsy Mae had the skill because her late husband had been an electrician.

He pursed his lips, frowning. "No, ma'am," he said again. "That's a different department. I take care of the main systems and minor repairs like this outlet. Plugged sinks, jammed doors, that kind of thing."

"Oh, good to know." Molly smiled. "My friend is staying here, and her microwave isn't working."

Reg adjusted his tool belt. "Have her call the front desk. They'll bring her a new one."

"I will. Thanks." Molly watched the repairman stride toward the ballroom doorway, then continued on with her loaded cart to the next table. "Scone?" she asked. "I have raspberry almond, lemon poppy seed, and classic cream with currants."

"I'll take a classic cream," one woman said. "It sounds yummy." She picked up a small scroll tied with ribbon, laid above her place setting. "What's this?"

"I have one too," another woman said. She slid off the ribbon and unrolled it. "Oh, it's a poem. Listen." She read a short, sweet poem out loud.

"One of the classes must have done them," the first woman said. She smiled up at Molly as she set a plate in front of her. "Thank you. It looks delicious."

The rest of the women at the table made their selections and Molly moved on to the next group, which included Madelaine Alt, her agent Caroline Callahan, Alyssa Martin, and a lean man with thick, gray hair. His name tag identified him as Joe Byers, the Highland Hearts editor.

"Scone?" she asked. "Baked fresh today."

But before she could list the flavors, Caroline screamed. She shoved back her chair and staggered to her feet as it toppled over. With a trembling finger, she pointed at the scroll on her plate. From where she stood, Molly could easily read what it said.

I know what you did.

10

Madelaine reached for the scroll and Molly barked, "Don't touch that!" When they all gaped at her, she said, "It might be evidence."

"Evidence of what?" Staring at the scroll as if it were a snake coiled on her plate, Caroline put a hand to her mouth. "I didn't do anything."

Then why had her reaction been so strong? Molly wondered. Who had left her the note? Did someone believe Caroline was involved in Gregory's death?

Fergus ran up to the table. "What's going on? Is there a problem with the food?"

"Caroline got a nasty note," Alyssa said. "It was on one of these scroll things." She picked up her own scroll and pulled off the ribbon. "Mine's okay."

"So is mine," Joe said. "Someone must have swapped your poem for that message, Caroline." He eyed the paper and ribbon. "The color of the ribbon is different. See?" Most of the ribbons were pale lavender. Caroline's was pink. Molly noticed name tents on the table and a reserved sign in a stand, so finding Caroline's seat had been simple.

Fergus read the scroll, careful not to touch the paper. "Who put these out?"

Madelaine shrugged. "One of your servers." She pointed across the room. "That young man, I believe. I saw him going around when I came in before tea." Her companions stared at her, and bright spots appeared in her cheeks. "Don't look at me. Why would I do such a thing? Caroline is my best friend."

The author had also been going around accusing people of murder. Maybe she had swapped the notes, her way of bringing attention to Caroline's possible guilt. *If* the note had to do with Gregory's death. It might refer to something else entirely.

"Were you in here until tea started?" Fergus asked Madelaine. Molly knew he was really asking if she had seen anyone else fiddle with the place settings.

Madelaine shook her head. "I'm afraid not. I nipped in for a second to search for a folder I'd left behind at lunch. That server was the lone person in here."

"Excuse me," Fergus said. "I'm going to go talk to him." On the way across the room, he paused at the microphones. "Hello, everyone. Please go back to your meal. Everything is fine. Something startled Ms. Callahan, that's all."

At this reassurance, the room began to hum with conversation and the clatter of dishes. Molly realized she had better get back to work herself. "So, who would like a scone?" she asked.

Despite doing her duty, Molly managed to circle around to stand near Caroline's table once Fergus returned with an update. "The server says he had a box full of the scrolls and he put them out randomly. He said they were all identical, with the purple ribbon."

"So someone sneaked in and swapped out Caroline's," Joe said. "Hence the pink ribbon." His hand flicked toward the center of the table, where Caroline had pushed the plate holding the offending message.

"I'd like to call the police," Fergus said. "They need to see that."

Caroline, seated now, leaned back to peer up at Fergus. "Why? Now that I've had time to think about it, I believe it's from a disgruntled author. I receive nasty notes all the time. Some people get angry when I tell them no."

Like Patsy Mae? But Molly didn't believe for a second that her friend had written that message. On the other hand, Caroline had treated her horribly, which was most likely a pattern. In Molly's experience, mean people rarely had only one victim.

Fergus studied Caroline, his brow creased. "I can't force you to turn it over to the police, of course, so I'm not going to try. But I'm going on record that I'm concerned." He gazed around the table. "And you all heard me say that."

He waited until everyone nodded, then pulled out his phone and bent close and snapped a photo. "I'm taking a picture of this, for the record. Unless you'll give it to me."

After he moved back, Caroline put her hand over the paper, not quite touching it. "No need. I'll dispose of it." She glanced at Molly. "I'd like another scone. Raspberry this time."

"Coming right up." Molly's cheeks burned at the realization that they all knew she'd been listening in. Well, what of it? Of course she was curious, especially since her old friend was still in the hot seat concerning Gregory's death.

She took away Caroline's empty plate and placed a fresh scone in front of her. "Anyone else need anything while I'm here? They're going fast."

Once everyone had eaten their fill, Molly and her friends sat down for a snack in the almost empty ballroom.

"Everything went great," Laura said. "Well, except for Caroline's outburst. At first I thought she'd found something wrong with the food."

"Your baking? Never," Carol said. "Molly, you were closest to Caroline. What happened?"

Molly told them about the note, then how Caroline had tried to downplay the whole situation. "She told Fergus that she often gets nasty notes from rejected authors and tried to blame it on one of them."

Patsy Mae gave a little snort. "I understand the temptation, believe me. Caroline is among the worst for writing really cold rejection letters. I'd rather hear, 'Sorry, not for me,' than, 'Don't quit your day job.' Or, 'I only take on writers with talent.'"

"Does she really say things like that?" Molly was appalled. "How cruel."

"I'm surprised you queried her then," Laura said with a shudder. "I wouldn't dare."

Patsy Mae regarded the contents of her teacup thoughtfully. "You always think you're going to be the exception. She represents the biggest author in my genre. I couldn't help but imagine what it would be like to be chosen by her."

"Being a writer sounds rough," Laura said. "It was bad enough dealing with reviews when I was a chef. But at least we had happy diners every day, so the critics were more or less easy to disregard."

"And we have tons of satisfied customers now," Molly said. Fortunately they had always gotten great reviews on social media. They worked hard to make sure everyone left the bakehouse happy.

"Yes, it is hard," Patsy Mae agreed. "The problem is that the agents and publishers can stop us from ever sharing our work with *our* customers—the readers. Unless we self-publish of course, which is always an option. At least we have that now." She sighed. "But like most people, I dream of seeing my book in stores, maybe even recommended by my favorite magazines."

"Don't let one unnecessarily cruel rejection stop that dream," Laura said. "Your books deserve to be published. You'll get that yes sooner or later."

Patsy Mae beamed. "Thanks, Laura."

Carol stretched with a yawn. "I need to get going. Harvey and I are cooking burgers on the deck." She looked around the table. "You're welcome to come eat with us. It's the first cookout of the summer."

"I'm in," Laura said with a laugh. "I was just thinking that I didn't know what to cook tonight."

Molly was on the verge of accepting Carol's offer when she saw Patsy Mae's face fall. "I'd love to go," Patsy Mae said. "But I have that meeting with Caroline. Maybe I should cancel it."

"No, don't," Molly said. "This is your opportunity to get some answers from her."

Patsy Mae traced a finger along the tablecloth. "I'd really like it if one of you could come with me as support. And a witness to whatever she says."

"I'll go," Molly offered. After the scene during tea, she wouldn't say no to another chance to watch and listen to Caroline. In light of Gregory's murder, she doubted the note was from a disgruntled author. Was Caroline hiding something?

"Oh, thank you, Molly," Patsy Mae enthused. "I wish I could repay the favor somehow."

Molly smiled. "You have a rental car, right? You can drive us over to Carol's afterward, then give me a ride home. We all came in the hearse this morning."

Patsy Mae nodded in agreement. "Perfect plan. I don't mind missing dinner here tonight. There's a talk I really don't care about hearing. Plus it will be good to get out for a while." She grimaced. "And go somewhere besides the police station."

"Speaking of which," Carol said. "Have you heard any more from the police?"

"No, thank goodness." Patsy Mae put a hand to her head in a dramatic gesture. She lowered her voice. "Mr. McNab assured me that they don't have enough evidence to arrest me. They didn't find my fingerprints on that tanning bed, for example. And why would they? I never even went in Gregory's room."

Maybe they hadn't found any fingerprints, period. Anyone who watched a crime show or read the news knew better than to leave fingerprints nowadays. Good thing for DNA evidence, which could be extracted from a strand of hair or skin cells. Until she'd learned about DNA, Molly hadn't realized how many traces a person left behind.

The women helped the servers finish cleaning up. Laura retrieved platters and other items that belonged to the bakehouse to take back to Bread on Arrival to wash. Then Laura and Carol left, with Molly and Patsy Mae planning to arrive at Carol's house around six.

"Are you ready, Molly?" Patsy Mae's expression was a blend of excitement and fear. "I'm so glad you're coming with me. Caroline is really intimidating."

"She sure is," Molly said. "But remember, she's a human being, like the rest of us. You don't need to be afraid of her or anyone else."

They ran into Fergus on the way through the lobby to the elevator. "Good afternoon," he said. "The tea went very well. The staff have heard lots of compliments about it."

"That is so good to hear," Molly said. "They devoured almost every crumb. And what the guests didn't eat, the servers did."

Fergus smiled at Patsy Mae. "How are you today, Patsy Mae?"

Patsy Mae fiddled with her necklace. "I'm fine, thank you. A little nervous, though. Molly and I are going up to meet with Caroline Callahan."

Fergus's eyes flashed with recognition. "Oh, Ms. Callahan. I hope she's over her upset regarding that note. I grilled the staff and they have no idea where it came from."

"I'm sure they didn't have anything to do with it," Molly said. "It had to be a guest at the conference." No one was within earshot, so she added, "I wonder if Caroline had something to do with Gregory. Maybe someone knows something. Or saw something."

Fergus gave a soft grunt. "If so, they need to come forward. I have it on good authority, namely Chief Thomson, that they aren't even close to an arrest yet." Worry creased his forehead. "I'd really like to see the situation resolved. Until it is, there's a cloud over the resort. I've already heard grumbles that people want to quit their jobs."

"I hope they don't," Molly said. She knew from discussions with Fergus how hard he had worked to put together a strong team. And as an employer herself, she had experienced the difficulty of finding good people that meshed with your business values. The bakehouse was extremely fortunate to have Bridget and Hamish. Both were hard workers, reliable, and trustworthy, plus the customers loved them.

"Me too," Fergus said, his tone mournful. Then he stepped aside. "Well, I won't keep you. I've got to check in on dinner prep."

With a nod, he went on his way. Molly pushed the button for the elevator. Caroline's suite was on the same floor as Patsy Mae and Gregory, she realized. Where had she been the afternoon Gregory was killed?

The doors opened and they stepped inside, to be whisked upward to their destination.

"I'm going to stop by my room and drop most of this off," Patsy Mae said when they emerged into the third-floor corridor. She had a tote full of books, conference materials, and other items.

Molly waited outside the room while Patsy Mae hurried in and dropped off her bag. She returned within moments, carrying only a folder and her phone. "Ready? Let's go."

The pair trudged down the quiet corridor, occasionally hearing voices or the murmur of a television in the rooms they passed. Many guests were resting before dinner, it seemed. But then Alyssa rushed toward them, her face tense and eyes focused straight ahead. Molly waved but she wasn't sure the woman noticed them, although she passed within inches.

"That was strange," Patsy Mae said, staring after Alyssa. "What was up with her?"

Molly shrugged. She couldn't begin to imagine what fresh drama Alyssa was reacting to this afternoon.

Caroline's room was at the end of the wing, about as far from Gregory's suite as one could get. In a stomach-churning reprise of the other day, the door stood slightly ajar. Molly glanced at Patsy Mae, who was staring at the opening.

"Go ahead, knock," Patsy Mae said between stiff lips.

"All right." Molly reached out and rapped on the door a few times.

Soft footsteps sounded, then the door was pulled open, revealing a room attendant wearing a Castleglen uniform and a name tag that said *Paula*. Her face brightened when she saw Molly and Patsy Mae. "Oh good. Maybe you can help me."

That wasn't at all what Molly was expecting to hear, but she and Patsy Mae stepped inside the suite, which was almost identical to Gregory's in style and furnishings. "Is Caroline Callahan here?" Molly asked. "The woman staying in this room?"

"I don't know, but come see this." Paula hastened toward a closed door. "I can't get inside the bathroom. The door opens a little, but then it gets stuck."

"Do you think Caroline is in there?" Molly felt the first trickle of concern. Maybe she'd fallen ill. "Did you see her today?"

"I haven't. Not since yesterday." The attendant took the knob and twisted, then pushed. "See? It opens an inch or so, but that's all." She released the knob and the door closed.

"Let me." Patsy Mae grunted as she took a turn. "I think the door budged a little more. There's definitely something blocking it." She tried again, this time using her shoulder. The door moved forward another few inches, enough to allow Patsy Mae to peek inside.

"Oh no," Patsy Mae cried. "It's Caroline!"

11

Her heart in her throat, Molly peeked through the partly open door. She couldn't see very much, only Caroline's feet and lower legs sprawled on the floor. The unresponsive literary agent had fallen in such a way as to prevent the door from opening.

Grabbing Patsy Mae by the arm, Molly gently tugged her away. "We can't do anything right now. She may have slipped getting out of the shower or something and injured her back. If we try to force the door open any further, we might hurt her."

Patsy Mae gnawed on her knuckles. "I feel so helpless. She's right there and we can't do anything."

Paula was pacing around, also obviously upset. "This is *awful*," she said, running a hand through her dark hair. "I should have known something was wrong."

"It's not your fault," Molly said. "For all you knew, the door got locked by accident, with no one inside." She ran to the side table and picked up the receiver, then dialed the front desk. "This is Molly Ferris. Please call an ambulance. And send Fergus up immediately," she said, giving the room number. "It's urgent. A guest is ill."

The clerk gasped softly. "Right away, Mrs. Ferris. I'll page him."

"Thank you." Molly hung up, grateful that help would be there soon.

Molly stood in a corner and Patsy Mae perched on a sofa while Paula paced the rug. Within minutes, Fergus rapped on the door, which was still open partway.

"What's going on?" he asked as he stepped inside.

Molly gave him a quick rundown, confirmed by the other two. "The front desk is calling 911," she finished.

Fergus went to the bathroom door and peered through the small opening, then he tipped his head to examine the door. "We need to get this off."

"Maybe Reg can do it," Molly said, eyeing the hinges. She noticed they were on the outside, which was smart. She imagined many a guest, perhaps even small children, had gotten locked inside one of the resort bathrooms.

"Not Reg," Fergus said. "He just quit." He stepped over to the room phone and called the front desk to ask for assistance.

"That's so strange about Reg," Paula said. "He was up here a little bit ago. I was working across the hall, and we said hello."

A trickle of cold sweat ran down Molly's spine at this news. Reg had quit—after visiting this very room. And now Caroline was ill or injured. As soon as Fergus hung up, she told him, "Reg was up here this afternoon."

"That's right," Paula put in. "I saw him. He said he was fixing the thermostat."

The expression on Fergus's face was grim. "That's not good. Who else did you see come to this suite, Paula? Anyone?"

The attendant nodded. "A man and a woman. I saw them while I was cleaning across the hall." In response to her boss's questions, she gave a description.

"That sounds like Alyssa Martin and Joe Byers," Molly said. "Which makes sense, since they're book editors."

"We'll need to talk to them." Fergus snatched up the phone again, and this time Molly heard him tell the clerk to call the police. "I may be jumping the gun," he said when he hung up. "But I don't like the fact that Reg took off after coming to this very room."

Another staff member arrived, and he and Fergus set to work removing the door. Paramedics entered soon after, joining Fergus inside the bathroom.

Molly, not wanting to watch, found herself pacing around the suite, much like the room attendant. Her gaze fell on the round table by the window. Several book manuscripts sat in a pile, and more out of idle curiosity than anything, she glanced at the top one. The author's name was Isla Tod.

"Patsy Mae, have you ever heard of Isla Tod?" Molly asked. It was a pretty name, if a bit old-fashioned.

"No, I haven't," Patsy Mae said. "She must be a new author." She got to her feet and came over to the table. But when she reached for the top page, which held only the author's name and the book title, Molly stopped her.

"We really shouldn't touch anything," Molly said. Maybe she was being overly cautious, but better that than disturb a piece of evidence.

Then she noticed that instead of loading Caroline onto a gurney, the paramedics were standing in the bathroom doorway. Fergus met her eyes and shook his head. Molly's knees weakened. She could guess what that meant.

Caroline was dead. But how? And why?

Fergus came over to the three women. "The police are going to want to talk to you, but I think you need to wait somewhere else."

The room attendant gasped, a hand going to her mouth. "The police? Is Ms. Callahan . . . " Her voice trailed off.

"I'm afraid so," Fergus said. He rubbed his chin, thinking. "Your room is nearby, Patsy Mae. Why don't you three go there? I'll see if the police can talk to you soon so you can go about your business."

"What about the rooms I need to clean?" Paula asked. "I didn't even get started on this one."

Molly's eyes met Fergus's. That was actually a stroke of luck. Once she vacuumed, all kinds of evidence would be gone.

"Don't worry about it," Fergus said. "I'll have someone else take over for you. You go with Molly and Patsy Mae, okay?"

The room attendant reluctantly trailed Patsy Mae and Molly down the corridor to the room, leaving her cart behind.

"I guess I'd better tell Carol that we'll be late," Molly said as Patsy Mae unlocked the door. Not that she was hungry. Quite the opposite, in fact, after discovering another sudden death. Had Caroline suffered from an ailment? Had a heart attack, maybe? Or was something more sinister at play? The knot in her stomach spoke to the latter.

"We can always grab dinner here later," Patsy Mae said. "Would you like a cold drink, Paula? I have water and iced tea. By the way, I'm Patsy Mae and this is Molly."

"Nice to meet you," Paula said brightly, then her mouth turned down. "Except for the circumstances. This whole thing is so upsetting."

"It certainly is." Molly pulled out a chair at the table. Nothing to do now but wait.

Paula broke the heavy silence that fell over the trio while they sipped iced tea. "You know those people who visited Caroline? They were arguing with her."

Molly locked eyes with Patsy Mae. This might be significant. "What about? Did you hear?"

The room attendant shook her head. "Not really. I was in and out of the room across the hall, and I heard raised voices. And then a few minutes later, a slammed door. I peeked out and saw the man and woman walking down the hall together."

"Make sure you tell the police that, okay?" Molly said. "Anything that you saw or heard might help."

Paula tilted her head, regarding Molly with curious eyes. "You sound like you know what you're talking about." Her eyes widened. "Oh, I recognize you. You're that woman who keeps solving murders around town. My coworkers told me about you."

Molly shifted in her seat, uncomfortable with the idea that people talked about her. "I have been involved in a few . . . situations," she finally said. "But it's totally by accident, I assure you."

Paula wrinkled her nose. "That must be a drag. Getting wrapped up with murders and all."

You have no idea. Molly pasted a smile on her face. Changing the subject, she asked, "Anyone want a cookie from the bakehouse?" She'd tucked a bag in her tote.

"I still can't get over Reg maybe being involved," Paula said, crunching on an Abernethy biscuit. Color flamed across her cheekbones. "I thought he was so good-looking. And tall. He kind of reminded me of that model who died, Gregory Gregg."

Molly considered Paula's remarks. Reg was tall and attractive, but certainly not in Gregory's league. But beauty was in the eyes of the beholder, she supposed.

Someone knocked on the door a couple of minutes later. Molly jumped up, hoping it was the police or Fergus—anyone who could give them an update.

Chief Thomson was at the door, along with Officer Anderson. "May we come in?" he asked politely.

"Please do," Molly said. She led the officers back into the room. "Chief, Officer Anderson, this is Paula. She's the room attendant who figured out something was wrong."

The chief nodded, then turned to Molly and Patsy Mae. "We'd like to talk to Paula alone. Do you mind waiting in the hall?"

Patsy Mae got right up, grabbing a bottle of water from the table. "Of course not. We'll be right outside. Won't we, Molly?"

Once they left the room, they walked toward the elevators, where several chairs were placed.

"I am so relieved," Patsy Mae said. "I figured they would want to talk to me first."

"Why?" Molly asked. "Paula got to Caroline's suite before us."

Patsy Mae sat back with a sigh. "Because once again, someone died on this same floor." She gave her friend a crooked smile. "I'm so glad you were with me all day this time. You're my alibi."

"And you're mine," Molly said, sitting in the adjacent chair. "Three other people also went to the room today. And those are just the ones that we know of."

"That's true. You know what's strange? Reg went to Gregory's suite, and so did Alyssa." Patsy Mae took a sip of water. "Maybe she hung around after Joe left. She was by herself when we saw her."

"You realize we're speaking as if it was murder," Molly said. "We don't know that yet."

Patsy Mae lifted her water bottle to her lips. "I have a bad feeling about it," she said before taking another swallow.

Thinking of their dinner date, Molly found her phone and sent a message to Carol. They weren't going to make it in time—that much was plain. She also wanted to give Carol and Laura an update about what had happened to Caroline.

A couple of minutes later, footsteps sounded along the corridor that heralded Fergus's arrival. "Are the police talking to Paula?" he asked as he reached Molly and Patsy Mae. At their nods, he said, "I figured as much. The crime scene team is working in Caroline's room right now."

"Crime scene team?" Molly asked. "Then it's a suspicious death." She said that last a trifle too loud, the horrible words echoing in the otherwise quiet corridor. "Sorry."

"What happened to her?" Patsy Mae asked, her expression horrified.

Fergus pressed his lips together. "It appears as though she had a reaction to hair dye. A very bad one."

"So it could have been an accident?" Molly said, relief trickling into her veins. That would be tragic, but much better than another murder.

The resort owner shifted his stance. "I'm afraid not. They're working on the theory that it was deliberate. Something about the nature of her reaction to the dye. Normal allergies aren't so severe."

Molly's spirits sagged again after the all too brief lift. "That's awful. And oddly enough, the same people went to the room. Reg and Alyssa. Of course, that might not mean anything."

"Oh, I'm afraid it does," Fergus said, that grim note back in his tone. "They are putting an all-points bulletin out on Reg Tod. The fact that he quit today of all days was too much of a coincidence for the police."

Molly agreed with this logic. Then something he said chimed in her mind. "Did you say Reg *Tod*?" The same last name as on the manuscript she'd seen.

"Yes I did," Fergus replied. "That's his name. Reginald Tod." His face was anguished. "How did I make such a mistake in judgment as to hire him?"

Molly's heart went out to Fergus. "You had no reason not to hire him. Reg was a very good handyman. And maybe he's innocent. Perhaps he left for another reason."

Fergus attempted a smile. "Bless you for saying that, Molly. I guess time will tell. I hope the police track him down in short order."

"Caroline had a manuscript on her table by a writer named Isla Tod," Molly said. "And no, I didn't touch it. I only read the cover page. Do you think Isla Tod is somehow related to Reg?"

Fergus shrugged. "Probably a coincidence." That wan smile

deepened a trifle. "Unless old Reg was writing novels on the side. But I find that idea rather far-fetched, don't you?"

Molly tried to imagine the handyman toiling away during his free time, penning a romance novel. She had to agree that the idea seemed ridiculous. Still, she planned to mention it to the police anyway. Cases had been solved with far smaller—and stranger—clues.

Patsy Mae's room door opened and Paula rushed out, moving at almost a trot. Then she saw the resort owner standing there and practically screeched to a halt. "They said I'm all set," she told him. "Now I can finish my room assignment."

Fergus shook his head. "Why don't you go on home? We'll pay you for the full shift."

"Really?" Paula's mouth hung open. "That's so nice of you." She wrapped her arms around herself with a shudder. "I keep thinking about that poor woman."

"Understandable," Fergus said, his tone sympathetic. "I am going to ask one thing of you, Paula."

"What is it?" Paula's tone conveyed that she'd willingly do whatever her boss asked.

"Don't talk to anyone about Caroline, please," Fergus said. "Not even with your friends or family. The police need time to notify Caroline's family. Plus, they need to move fast to solve this case. Any gossip might help a criminal."

"I wouldn't want that." Paula nodded her head rapidly. "You can count on me, Mr. MacGregor." She ran pinched fingers across her mouth. "My lips are sealed."

"Thanks for understanding." Fergus moved to the elevator and pressed the button for his employee. "You have a good night, Paula."

The room attendant hurried into the elevator, giving them a quick wave before the doors closed.

Patsy Mae's door opened to reveal Officer Anderson. "Molly, can you please come in?"

Molly rose to her feet. "Guess I'm up. See you in a few."

"I'll be around all evening," Fergus said. "We could grab a bite to eat before you go home if you want."

"That would be nice," Molly said. "Patsy Mae and I were supposed to go to Carol's for dinner, but obviously that plan has been canceled. We'll come find you later."

Greer held the door open for Molly. "Have a seat," the officer said. "This won't take long."

Molly sat at the table across from Chief Thomson. "I'm ready," she told him.

The chief eyed her for a moment then said, "I understand you called in the incident. Can you take us through why you were in Caroline's room and exactly what occurred?"

Molly clasped her hands together in her lap. This was far from the first time she had been questioned by the police, and it never got any easier. "I'll be glad to, Chief," she said. "I remember every moment as if it has been branded in my brain. But there is one thing I want to mention first so it doesn't get lost. I think that, in light of what has happened, it is probably relevant."

Both officers looked at her, interest on their faces.

"Earlier today, during the high tea event, Caroline got a note. At first I thought it was a taunt." Molly swallowed hard. "But now I think maybe it was a threat."

12

"How is Patsy Mae doing?" Carol asked Molly in the bakehouse kitchen the next morning. "The poor thing must be beside herself after discovering two people she was supposed to meet with murdered."

"She's actually doing okay, believe it or not." Molly grabbed a mug and filled it with fresh, fragrant coffee. "I'm glad that Fergus and I could spend time with her last night." Patsy Mae had ended up eating at King's Heid Pub with Fergus and Molly. A hearty and delicious dinner had restored their spirits.

Laura emerged from the walk-in cooler with her arms full of ingredients. "I can't believe it was the handyman," she said. "What possible motive could he have?"

Molly added a splash of milk to her mug. "He may have been a disgruntled author, I suppose. But that doesn't explain why Gregory was killed. He was only a model, not an editor or agent. He didn't have any publishing power."

"If they think it was him, then they'll have to figure out what the connection is." Carol wandered over to the coffee and filled her mug. "Unless he was a hit man, paid off by someone."

Laura wrinkled her nose. "A hit man? I think that's a stretch."

Molly giggled at the idea of the lanky, laconic Reg working as a paid assassin. No, it certainly didn't fit. But neither did the idea that he had killed Gregory and Caroline, even for personal reasons. And if so, what had connected the pair besides the industry they worked in?

"Well, maybe you're right," Carol said. "But I can't think of a theory that makes the pieces fit together."

"Me neither," Molly admitted. "I think we need to do some background research." She glanced at the clock. "After the morning rush."

The first couple of hours were busy, with people stopping in for breakfast and to grab coffee on the way to work. Around ten or so, the stream of customers thinned and Bridget arrived for a shift, allowing Molly to sit down with her laptop. After setting the computer up on a table in the café, she selected a slightly misshapen but still near-perfect scone from Laura's discard pile and refilled her mug.

Carol, carrying a snack of her own, slid into the chair opposite. "Where do we begin?" she asked. She bit into a raspberry turnover that showered flakes of pastry onto her plate. "Wow, this is good. Worth the mess."

"I can't remember Laura making anything I didn't think was worth the mess. Or the calories." Molly rested her fingers on her keyboard. "I'm going to see what I can find out about our runaway repairman."

"Runaway repairman," Carol mused. "I like that."

Carol wasn't alone, nor was Molly especially original. After entering Reg's name into the search bar, a list of headlines immediately popped up. *Runaway Repairman Flees Murder Scene*, screamed one tabloid publication.

Molly scanned the articles quickly, wondering if they would reveal any insights about Reg's life. "Aha," she said. "Reg was from Harvey, Michigan."

Carol dabbed at her mouth with a napkin. "Laura was born in Harvey." Laura had lived in the small town until age ten, when her parents moved to the Marquette house they still lived in.

As if on cue, Laura entered from the kitchen holding a tray of fresh toffee-chip shortbread. Carol gestured her over.

"Right after I unload these," Laura said. She set down the tray and opened the case, then carefully added the cookies to the display. "Are you okay right now?" she asked Bridget.

The college student nodded, her trademark smile in place. "I'm fine. I'll holler if I need help."

Laura finished with the cookies and came around the side of the counter to join the others. She pulled a chair from another table and sat. "What's up?"

"Reg Tod is from Harvey," Molly said. "Did you know his family?" She searched for Reg Tod and Harvey together. "I found some obituaries." She opened the latest, for a Darlene Tod. "His mother, Darlene, died. Oh, and his father, Rufus. That's sad."

"None of those names ring a bell," Laura said. "But I'm about a decade older than Reg, so he wouldn't have been part of my childhood circle." She pulled her phone out of her apron pocket. "But maybe Mom or Dad remembers them. I'll ask."

"Good thinking," Carol said.

Rather than text her parents, Laura called them, then shook her head. "Voice mail." She left a message asking them to call her back soon because she had a question.

"I'm not finding much else about Reg," Molly said. He'd kept a very low profile online. She didn't find any social media accounts, any articles mentioning him, or even an entry in the Harvey police log. Needing a breather, she picked up her mug.

"While you have your computer on, why don't we look up Gregory Gregg and Caroline?" Laura suggested. She tapped the table. "Let me know what you find out. I'm going to get back to work."

Molly set her mug down. "That's a good idea. It can't hurt to know more about them." She typed *Gregory Gregg biography* into the search bar. Dozens, if not hundreds, of pages came up. With his recent death, he was all over the Internet.

But Molly clicked on his personal web page, wanting to go to the source rather than possibly inaccurate articles. She scanned *About Gregory* quickly, the lead-in talking about the many covers he'd done and the fact that he was a fan favorite. One quote said he was, "the Scottish Fabio."

At the bottom, a brief paragraph talked about his life before modeling. "Oh, listen to this," Molly exclaimed. "Gregory was a naturalized Scottish citizen, but he was born in Michigan."

"I did not know that," Carol said. "Where?"

"It doesn't say." Molly went over it again to make sure she hadn't missed anything. "No, it just says Michigan."

"Maybe he wanted to keep his family out of the limelight," Carol suggested. "Or perhaps they didn't approve of his modeling career."

Molly couldn't imagine that since Gregory Gregg had been quite wealthy, judging by the pictures of him at home in a grand manor in the Scottish countryside. But she could understand not wanting to be constantly scrutinized by the press. It was bad enough being mentioned when she and her friends were involved in a case.

"On to Caroline," Molly said, typing the woman's name into the search engine. The literary agent had kept a very low profile. She had her own agency, and the company's site included a brief bio mentioning well-known clients—notably Madelaine Alt—and her Connecticut upbringing. She'd gone to Smith College.

Not satisfied, Molly returned to the search results and clicked another link to a recent article featuring the agent and her famous client, Madelaine. "This looks interesting," Molly told Carol, then gave her the highlights.

The article focused on how Caroline, a new agent at the time, had discovered Madelaine in the so-called slush pile. She'd fought to sell Madelaine's book, receiving many rejections from editors. Then Tartan and Lace, a new imprint, had taken it on.

"And basically the rest is history," Molly concluded. "Madelaine is a best-selling author and Caroline was noted for discovering fresh talent."

"Fascinating," was Carol's verdict. "A real success story for the two of them."

"And now one of them is dead." Molly stared at the computer screen but she wasn't really seeing it anymore. "What did Caroline do that made someone that angry?"

The door to the bakehouse burst open, revealing a large group of chattering women. Where had they come from? Molly glanced into the parking lot and saw a tour bus. She closed her browser and shut down her computer. They'd have to wait until later to continue their investigation. Duty called.

Patsy Mae phoned Molly as the bakehouse door closed behind the bus tour. "Are you three coming over later? Tonight we're having a cookout with sword fighting demonstrations and a performance by The Leaping Lowlanders."

"That does sound fun," Molly said. "We'll come out after we close this afternoon. I bet Carol will bring Harvey too." She thought for a second, then asked, "Who is doing the sword fighting?"

"The male models." Patsy Mae sighed. "It's such a shame we lost Gregory. He was the absolute best."

Molly guessed that being a handsome face wasn't enough to make it as a male romance model. "What else do they do? Ride horses?"

"Indeed they do," Patsy Mae said. "A lot of them play Highland warriors in film and television too."

"I suppose they need to do whatever they can to make ends meet,"

Molly said. Now that Gregory was gone, would another model rise to become the "Scottish Fabio"?

Fortunately the afternoon was quite slow, with many people either working or out enjoying the gorgeous weather. The lull gave Molly and the others time to catch up with other tasks, including ordering inventory, doing the bookkeeping, and deep cleaning the kitchen and front service area.

After closing, Molly changed into jeans, a lightweight sweater, and sneakers. The cookout was casual, so everyone except the performers would be in regular clothing. And since the event was outdoors, Angus was welcome. "I feel like I've neglected you terribly," she told her sweet dog as they got into her silver Honda Fit. "I'm going to take you for a long walk around the resort grounds, I promise."

Angus gave a joyful bark in response. He was very familiar with the route to the resort, and he whined happily when they turned through the gateposts.

Molly found a spot at the rear of the lot near Laura's Volkswagen and Carol's Chrysler. She also recognized vehicles that belonged to The Leaping Lowlanders, including Bridget's. Molly marveled at the college student's endless supply of energy—not only was Bridget working extra hours at the bakehouse this week, but she would also certainly deliver a standout dance performance tonight.

After leashing Angus, Molly strolled along a paved path to the rear of the main building, where cookouts and other outdoor festivities were held. The fragrant aroma of roasted meat drifted her way from huge grills, and she could see people milling around on the patio and the lawn. Jaunty umbrellas had been raised over the patio tables.

As Molly approached the patio area, she saw her friends, including Harvey, seated at a table. Patsy Mae spotted her first and waved.

"We ordered you an iced tea," Patsy Mae said, tugging out a metal chair for Molly to sit in.

"Thanks," Molly said, taking her seat. Angus had recognized Patsy Mae and was dancing about on his hind legs at her feet.

Patsy Mae patted him with a laugh, then ruffled his ears. "What a good boy you are." His response was a brief yip that drew smiles from people seated around them.

"He loves compliments," Molly said, picking up her glass. She took a long, refreshing sip. "What a beautiful afternoon for this event."

"It sure is," Harvey said. "I was fishing most of the day until this woman dragged me off my boat." He glanced at his wife with a chuckle.

Carol patted his knee. "Don't blame me. It was the prospect of dinner here at the resort that made you hang up your pole."

"Nonsense," he replied, giving her a quick peck on the cheek. "How could I say no to dinner out with my bride?"

"You two are so sweet together." Patsy Mae sighed. "Oh, how it brings back the memories."

"I remember Bo from your wedding," Harvey said. "He was a fine fellow."

Patsy Mae accepted his words with a tiny nod. "Thank you. I was a very lucky woman." She inhaled deeply. "But enough of that. I'm so happy to be here with y'all. We'll have to make it a regular thing."

"We should," Laura said. "How about we come to Louisiana next time?" She lifted her glass. "Girls' trip coming right up, preferably in the dead of winter when it's freezing cold here."

"Hey, now," Harvey protested. "You're going to leave an old man behind to shovel snow?"

"Yes," the Bakehouse Three chorused, then laughed.

Fergus approached the table. "Good afternoon, everyone," he said. He eyed the sun, which was slowly lowering over the lake. "Or should I say good evening?"

"Either is fine with me," Harvey said. "We're enjoying your fine hospitality."

"And I'm glad," Fergus said. "We have a wonderful turnout tonight. Not only conference guests, but a lot of locals from Loch Mallaig." He smiled and waved at Mayor Tavish Calhoun, who was approaching the patio with his wife, Sandra.

Molly wondered if people were here to see the Lowlanders and the sword fighting or if they were curious about the two murders. Probably a mix of both. She knew that it was human nature to be fascinated by tragedy and crime.

Angus bumped her leg with his head and she reached down to pat him. But when he did it a second time, she got the message. She stood up. "I think Angus is asking for that walk I promised him," she told her friends.

"Want some company?" Fergus asked. "I have time if we go right now."

"That works out perfectly," Molly said, secretly glad for the opportunity to spend some time with Fergus. "Because he's telling me we shouldn't wait."

Everyone laughed. "How cute that you know what your dog is thinking," Patsy Mae said.

"I wish that worked as well with husbands," Harvey commented to more laughter. "Sometimes Carol just doesn't get the message."

"Use your words," Carol said, tapping him gently in the chest. "I've told you I'm not a mind reader."

"My Bo was like that too," Patsy Mae said. "One time . . ."

Patsy Mae's voice blended into the general noise of the crowd as Molly, Fergus, and Angus made their way off the patio. "Your friend is sweet," Fergus said. "You can tell she really loved her husband."

"She really did," Molly said. "I wish I'd kept in better touch with her over the years. I met Bo at their wedding, then saw him again at a reunion years ago. He was a good man."

"Sounds like it," Fergus said. "Which way do you want to go?" They were standing near a fountain at a junction of several paths that wound through the grounds.

In one direction, the loch glittered, beckoning to Molly. "Let's walk by the lake. It's such a perfect day for it."

"Agreed," Fergus said. They set off, strolling in silence as they took in the beautifully landscaped gardens and lawns. A distance away, golf carts trundled about the manicured greens. "I don't get out and enjoy this property enough. I'm always so busy, even with Neil helping me."

"Where is Neil?" Molly asked. "I haven't seen him around."

"He's out of town at a hospitality conference," Fergus said. He grunted a laugh. "And boy, I could have used him this week."

"I'm sure," Molly said. On top of the usual responsibilities, Fergus had been dealing with two deaths on the property. Having his son around certainly would have eased the pressure. "How are you doing?"

Fergus didn't answer for a long moment, seeming to be considering his words. "I'm okay," he finally said. "Sad, of course. For the victims and their families. But remaining hopeful that the police will identify the culprit quickly. Or *culprits*." He paused. "Naturally one worries about the effect on a business when this kind of thing happens. But bookings are actually up."

Molly shook her head. "People are like that, fascinated by the scene of the crime. And both victims were pretty high profile this time."

"I can't relate to that mindset," Fergus said. "Not at all." He turned his blue-eyed gaze on her. "And what about you? Once again you're neck-deep in a case."

"Not because I wanted to be, believe me," Molly said. "But on the other hand, I'm glad I can support Patsy Mae. She managed to blunder into both situations, purely by coincidence of course. Madelaine sure seems eager to blame her for Gregory's death."

Fergus made a scoffing sound. "Patsy Mae wouldn't hurt a flea. Anyone with eyes can see that."

They had reached the lakefront and were now skirting the water on a groomed path. Motorboats buzzed across the loch while others rocked gently on their anchors as fishermen waited for a bite. Several kayaks glided across the glassy water in tandem like a school of colorful fish.

Falling silent again, they walked along the curving path, which conformed to the shape of the shore. Around a corner, Molly saw a wooden building constructed so it extended over the water. "What's that?" she asked, never having ventured this way.

"It's the old boathouse," Fergus said. "After we built new docks, we stopped using it. It's only big enough for one motorboat and a few canoes and kayaks."

"Can we go inside?" Molly asked. She loved to explore old buildings, and this rustic structure was charming, with an overhanging roof and peeled bark railings.

"Sure thing," Fergus said, patting his pocket. "I still have the padlock key on my ring." He pulled out a handful of keys attached to a metal hoop. "I keep thinking I should throw most of these away, but I never get around to it."

"I know what you mean," Molly said. "I still have stray keys from my place in Chicago." She thought about tossing them whenever she came across them, but never did. They felt like a connection to the past.

Fergus flicked through the ring, giving a hoot of satisfaction when he found the correct key. Holding it between his fingers, he led Molly and Angus around the building. They were right behind him when he stopped short, almost causing Molly to crash into him.

"What on earth?" he exclaimed.

Molly stepped to one side so she could see what he was talking about. The padlock hung from its hasp, meaning someone had broken into the boathouse.

Was the trespasser still inside?

13

"Wait here. I need to check this out." Fergus strode down the moss-spotted concrete path to the doorway.

Angus yipped and pulled Molly forward. "Be careful," she called. "There might be someone in there."

Fergus threw a glance over his shoulder. "I sure hope not, for their sake. It's not very safe for anyone to be inside if they don't know the place." Nevertheless, he pushed the door open and disappeared into the dark interior.

Disregarding his request to stand back, Molly hastened after Fergus, worried that someone might be lurking and attack him. She paused in the doorway, restraining Angus, who was still pulling on the leash. The inside of the building was lit by high windows, with very little light coming through at this time of day. In the center, water gleamed black, giving off a dank, fishy scent. This was where boats were once moored, the big double doors giving ready access to the lake. Around three sides of the open area were walkways, and Molly saw old life preservers and oars hung on the plank walls.

Fergus was over in the rear back corner, shining his phone's flashlight on what appeared to be a heap of old tarps. "I think someone has set up camp in here."

Molly edged along the walkway, careful to keep Angus close. He kept darting toward the water as if he wanted to jump in, but she kept him away from it. In the corner, tarps and an old blanket had been arranged in the shape of a bed, with a faded orange life jacket for a pillow. A paper sack held food wrappers and an empty water bottle.

"Who could be staying here?" Molly found herself whispering. "Do you think it might be Reg Tod?" That seemed like a logical assumption, since the man had disappeared from the resort and hadn't been seen since.

"That's a good bet," Fergus said. "I'm going to have the police take a look. And I'll replace the lock as well. I can't have people camping out on the property." He dialed a number on his phone. "Hi, Chief," he said in greeting. "It's not an emergency, but I may have a lead on our fugitive." He explained the situation, then hung up.

"Is someone coming over?" Molly asked.

Fergus nodded, then gestured in the direction of the resort's main building. "You don't need to wait here with me, Molly. Go ahead back to your friends."

Despite the logic of his suggestion, Molly was strangely reluctant to leave. For one thing, she was curious to see what the police thought. Plus, she didn't want to leave Fergus here alone. What if the trespasser came back? Not that she could do much to protect him, but she felt compelled to stay all the same.

"I'll wait," she said, wrapping her spare arm around her middle. She was freezing, she realized. "But how about out in the sunshine? It's so damp and chilly in here."

"Watch your step," Fergus cautioned, then followed her out.

Once Molly stepped into the sunshine, the strong rays quickly penetrated her chilled bones. "Much better," she said.

Lowering his sunglasses from his hair, Fergus stood with arms folded across his chest, studying the glittering water. "This is so nice. I wish we could store summer in a bottle for winter."

"Me too," Molly said, her tone heartfelt. The Upper Peninsula was beautiful in the winter, but the season was long and often difficult to endure.

By unspoken agreement, they chatted about the weather and other inconsequential topics while they waited for the police to arrive. Fergus had a great knack for telling stories, and his anecdotes about the inner workings of the resort made Molly laugh. In turn, he was a good listener when Molly bounced a couple of ideas off him regarding marketing for the bakehouse.

Molly was almost disappointed when a cruiser came bouncing down the lane to the boathouse. The vehicle drew to a halt and Chief Thomson and Officer Anderson got out. "We came in through the golf course," the chief said by way of greeting. "We didn't want to alarm the partygoers at the cookout."

"That was thoughtful of you," Fergus said. "Come on. I'll show you what we discovered."

Knowing there wasn't much room on the narrow catwalk to maneuver, Molly remained outside with Angus. She went down to a small, sandy area adjacent to the boathouse and allowed him to get his feet wet.

The trio emerged from the boathouse quickly, Chief Thomson leading the way. "This could definitely be our man," he was saying. "There hasn't been any sign of Tod or his vehicle since you reported that he'd quit."

The fact that Reg seemed to be in hiding didn't speak well to his possible innocence. But then again, being falsely accused of murder was a scary prospect. Molly was sure that hiding was a strong temptation.

"We'll certainly keep an eye out for him," Fergus said. "And I'm going to have the lock changed on the door." He pulled the padlock out of the hasp. "And use one of those padlocks that can't be cut as easily."

Officer Anderson took the padlock from Fergus to examine it. "That wasn't cut, which must mean the person had a key. Did Reg have access to keys?"

"Yes," Fergus confirmed, then pulled out his key ring. "I usually leave this in my office in case a staff member needs it. We've mostly transitioned to new locks, but there are a few oldies still."

"So Reg could have made copies," Greer said. "But it sounds like other people might have as well."

Fergus grimaced. "I know. That's why I started carrying this ring around. Maybe it's too late, but it makes me feel a little better."

"We can station an officer or two here tonight if you want," Chief Thomson said. "They can make regular circuits of the property, especially down here along the lakefront." His gaze swept a nearby grove of trees. "It's such a big place. Reg Tod could be lurking anywhere right now."

"I might take you up on that," Fergus said, his brows knitting together in concern. "I hate to be an alarmist, but there's a good chance Reg did bunk here."

"And since he's wanted for questioning in two murders," Officer Anderson added, "an officer on-site is an excellent idea. We'll also take a look around before we go."

Put that way, Molly had to agree with the officers. "I think we'll all feel safer," she said, but then a terrible thought struck. Maybe Reg wasn't sticking around the resort to evade capture. Maybe he had another victim in his sights.

As if reading her mind, Fergus said, "I'm going to have a quiet word with those who were closest to Gregory and Caroline. They'll need to be extra cautious until we locate Reg."

"He can't get into the main building or the rooms, right?" Greer asked.

"That's correct," Fergus said. "After he left, we changed all the codes for the rooms, plus we always lock the entrances at night. You need a key to get in unless you come through the lobby. We also have a vast camera network."

"Good protocol," Officer Anderson said. "I'd also warn the staff to safeguard any master keys. Make sure those are secured when they are off duty."

"We already do." Fergus patted his pocket. "This was a loophole that is now closed."

Chief Thomson promised to have an officer arrive for duty immediately, then he and Officer Anderson left to patrol the property. Fergus called for someone to bring down a lock, and a few minutes later, a golf cart buzzed along the lane to the old boathouse.

To Molly's surprise, Neil was driving. "Hey Dad," he said, hopping down from the cart. "I heard you had a little excitement around here while I was gone."

"Understatement of the year." Fergus clapped his son on the shoulder. "Glad you're back. Let's get the new lock installed." He threw Molly a smile. "Or else Molly here will be late for dinner."

"Can't have that," Neil said cheerfully. "How are you, Molly?"

"I'm fine, thank you," Molly replied.

While waiting for Fergus and Neil to change the padlock, she walked a restless Angus a short distance away, to the fringe of the woods. A rising breeze tossed the treetops with a pleasant rustling sound, and Molly tipped her head to watch the movement of the leaves.

In the depths of the woods, a branch snapped with a loud crack. Angus barked.

Molly's peace and contentment fled, replaced by a shiver of fear. Was Reg Tod in those woods? Had he been watching and listening to them all this time?

"Come on, Angus. Let's go." Molly pulled gently on his leash, but the little dog stood rooted in place, staring into the woods. His ears twitched, and he barked again. There was definitely something out there. Most likely an animal, but still . . .

"Are you ready, Molly?" Fergus called. "We're all set here."

"Want me to give you a ride?" Neil asked. "There's room."

"Sure," Molly said as she walked back, eager to return to other people. She picked up Angus and climbed into the rear seat of the golf cart.

"You don't have to sit back there, Molly," Fergus protested. "The front seat is more comfortable."

Molly waved away his concern. "Don't be silly. I know you and Neil need to catch up on business."

"We do," he admitted. "Are you sure you don't mind?"

"Not in the least," Molly said.

"Dad, you're the one who taught me not to argue when a lady insists," Neil chimed in.

Fergus laughed and swung into the front seat.

"Ready?" Neil asked. At their assent, he set off down the lane, the cart motor humming.

Molly sat back against the seat and tried to enjoy the ride, but she found herself scanning the property for any sign of Reg. Was he lurking behind that row of hedges? Or in the shadow of a toolshed? Realizing that her fingernails were gripping the edge of her seat, she forced herself to let go. Reg, if he was here, wasn't interested in her or any of her friends. She had nothing to worry about.

Carol and the others were playing a game of badminton when the golf cart approached the patio, and they stopped to watch as Neil halted to let Molly and Angus out.

"I'll see you later, Molly," Fergus said. "Neil and I need to make the rounds."

"Sounds good," Molly said. "See you soon." She led Angus across the grass to her friends.

"Where have you been?" Carol asked. "We were starting to get worried."

Molly made sure no one else was in earshot before she said a word. She didn't want to be responsible for creating a panic. "Fergus and I walked down to the old boathouse. It looks like someone has been staying there."

"Who?" Laura asked. Her eyes widened. "Oh, I get it. Reg Tod."

"Exactly," Molly said. "Of course, it's only a theory right now. Fergus called the police anyway. The chief and Greer came to check it out." She saw the familiar figure of Deputy Chief Broderick Gillespie on the fringe of the crowd. He was dressed in street clothes, likely so his presence wouldn't alarm the guests. She nodded in his direction. "And they've stationed an officer here for the evening."

"We'd better stick together then," Patsy Mae said nervously. "He could be anywhere."

Harvey frowned. "Maybe we should head home, Carol. I don't like the idea of running into a fugitive from the law. He might be dangerous."

Carol made a dismissive sound. "We're not in any danger, Harvey. Why would Reg bother us? We don't even know him."

"That's what I've been telling myself," Molly said. "And I'm sure that if he's here, Fergus and the police will find him." She glanced at the badminton net. "I'd love to play a game if we have time before dinner."

"We sure do," Harvey said, swinging his racket. "Grab another person and you two can play the winner of this game."

Joyce Bruce was nearby, so Molly asked her to join. For the next half hour or so, they focused on batting birdies over the net and trying to score the most points. Angus, of course, thought it was all great fun and tried to chase the shuttlecocks, so Molly had to tie him to a post.

Afterward, they surrendered the net to another group and got in line at the buffet. Tonight's menu offered a choice of hamburgers or chicken accompanied by an array of cold salads. Molly chose chicken, potato salad, and a green bean salad with cherry tomatoes and feta cheese.

Bridget appeared from the main building, dressed in her Leaping Lowlanders outfit, and walked up to their table. "Hi, everyone," she said with a wave.

"Go grab something and sit with us," Molly said. They were seated at a table for eight, and even with Joyce and Hamish joining their group, there was room for Bridget.

"Maybe I will." Bridget put a hand to her belly. "Something light, though. I don't like to eat too much before I dance." Her eyes widened as she took in the food-laden tables. "Who are all those tall, handsome men in kilts at the buffet?"

Laura laughed. "Those are the male cover models," she said. "They're doing a sword fighting demo later."

Bridget wagged a finger with a smile. "You've been holding out on me, ladies. Leaving me to slave at the bakehouse while you enjoyed the conference." They all laughed at her teasing. "Save that seat," she said. "I'll be right back."

The fresh air and exercise had given Molly an appetite, and she ate heartily. The chicken breast was juicy and tender, flavored with a tangy barbecue sauce, and the salads were perfectly seasoned. "I love this green bean salad," she said, spearing the last crisp bean. "I'm going to make it at home."

"It is tasty." Laura scooped up a forkful of the same salad and chewed thoughtfully. "I can taste balsamic vinegar, olive oil, and a hint of garlic powder and ground mustard."

"Laura, our resident recipe whisperer," Carol said. "You're amazing."

Laura accepted the compliment with a nod. "It's a professional habit, for sure. When I was a chef, we used to try to reconstruct recipes made by other people all the time. Either to inspire us or to figure out what doesn't work so well."

"Let me tell you about this hamburger," Harvey said. He chewed a bite, eyes gazing upward, then swallowed. He dabbed his mouth. "The beef was well-salted, seasoned with Worcestershire sauce, paprika, basil, and brown sugar."

Laura laughed. "Despite that teasing twinkle in your eye, Harvey, you're spot-on."

"Brown sugar?" Hamish eyed his burger with surprise. "I never thought of putting sugar in ground beef."

"Me neither," Harvey said. "But it works, doesn't it?"

Patsy Mae laughed. "Before I head home, I'm going to make a pot of Bo's jambalaya. Y'all can deconstruct that, see how close you get."

"Yum," Molly said. "I love Cajun cooking. Will you give us the recipe?"

Patsy Mae pretended to think about it. "If you ask me nicely. It's one of my go-tos. I make it for church suppers all the time."

"I have a couple of those recipes," Carol said. "They're crowd-pleasing favorites."

"Ooh, tell me," Patsy Mae replied. As Carol launched into a description of a signature dish, Molly saw Fergus walk out onto the patio. He stopped and searched the crowd. Spotting her, he wove his way toward their table.

"Dinner is wonderful," Molly told him when he arrived. "Are you going to eat?"

"Later." He hunched down, one hand resting on the back of her chair. "We have a problem," he said in a low voice. "Some of the security cameras aren't working, and we have no idea exactly when they malfunctioned. Or why."

Molly frowned. "You mean someone might have sabotaged them?"

"It's a possibility. And that would mean they're planning on doing something they don't want anyone to see." Fergus's expression was grim. "Something bad."

14

Molly absorbed the implications of this news. Maybe the camera issues had nothing to do with Reg Tod, but she found that hard to believe. Had the talented handyman tampered with them to hide his movements? She pictured him slipping in and out of the main building undetected. If he still had a resort uniform, many guests wouldn't give him a second glance.

"What's next?" she asked. "Do you know yet?"

"We're going to do a sweep of the main building," Fergus said. "The officers are going to enter each and every room. I've suggested they do it out of uniform as I'd like to prevent a panic."

"By the looks of this crowd, I'd say most of your guests are out here," Molly observed.

"I think so too," Fergus said. "But I'm sure some rooms will be occupied." He rose to his feet. "I'll let you get back to your meal. But I thought you might want an update."

"Thanks, I appreciate that." Molly thought of one room that might be occupied, even though it shouldn't be. No, make that two. "I think you should check Gregory and Caroline's rooms. If I were lurking about, I might use one of those since they're empty right now, right?"

Fergus appeared impressed. "Good thinking, Molly. In fact, we'll go there first." He tapped the table. "See you in a while."

"What's going on?" Carol asked when he'd left. "Anything new?"

Molly checked the people nearby to be sure no one was paying attention. The lively fiddle music from a pair playing in one corner of the patio was also providing effective cover for their conversation. "Fergus and the police are going to search the building. Just to make sure our fugitive isn't hiding somewhere." She didn't mention the faulty cameras. The less said about that the better. Hopefully they would get them back online quickly.

Patsy Mae fanned a hand in front of her face. "And to think that I thought this conference might be boring. It's been anything but."

"It's all a little too exciting for my taste," Harvey said. "I retired from investigative journalism in the hopes my life would be boring. I'll be happy when they find that guy and things go back to normal."

Carol patted his arm. "It won't be long, I'm sure. Are you ready for dessert?"

Harvey pushed back his chair and chuckled. "When am I ever not ready for dessert?"

After dinner, The Leaping Lowlanders performed for the group, dancing on the lawn near the patio. One of the troupe's principal dancers, Bridget shone in her spotlighted role, her sunny smile bright and unwavering.

Fergus hadn't returned by the time the dancers took their final bows. To be sure she hadn't missed him, Molly got up and wandered through the crowd. She knew a number of the attendees from Loch Mallaig and stopped to say hello, but all the while, anxiety churned in her stomach. Had they found Reg Tod? Was he even on the property? It was entirely possible that they were wrong and he was miles away from here by now.

When Molly made it back to her table, she still hadn't seen Fergus. The editor Joe Byers was seated in Bridget's seat—and Angus was in Harvey's, resting his nose on Carol's lap. Molly saw Harvey, Hamish, and Joyce standing a short distance away, talking to Alastair Thomson and the mayor.

Joe stood as she approached, extending his hand. "I don't believe we've officially met." The editor was dressed in a kilt, as he had been every other time Molly had seen him.

After introductions, Molly sat, and Patsy Mae said, "Joe loved my book. He wants to talk to me about publishing it."

"That's wonderful," Molly said, barely suppressing a squeal of excitement. "Congratulations to both of you."

Joe grinned. "I was up most of the night reading Patsy Mae's book. It was totally enthralling. One of the best I've read in some time. You're a true talent, Patsy Mae."

With each compliment, Patsy Mae's face turned a deeper shade of pink. Her smile was wide enough to make her cheeks ache. "I can't thank you enough, Joe. Do you know how long I've waited to hear those words?" At this, she choked up, blinking furiously. Laura handed her a tissue.

"This is one of the best parts of the job," Joe said. "Saying yes to an author. I know how hard it is to put yourself out there and field all those rejections. It can be soul crushing. But the fact of the matter is that there are more writers than available slots."

"And I now have one of those slots." Patsy Mae shook her head in disbelief, then sniffed and blew her nose.

"Should Patsy Mae get an agent?" Laura asked.

Joe tapped his fingers on the table. "I advise my writers to do so. Agents help negotiate the contract, plus handle a lot of tasks that writers aren't necessarily well versed in doing."

"I queried Caroline a few times," Patsy Mae said. "That might go without saying. She was one of the biggest in the business."

"Yes, she was," Joe agreed. "It's a real loss to the industry."

But something about his expression told Molly that he wasn't being totally sincere. "What is it, Joe?" she asked. "Did you have issues with

Caroline? I know others did." She looked at Patsy Mae, wondering if she'd share her experience.

Patsy Mae nodded. "Something happened with Caroline and another book I was querying," she said. "I won't go into details, but I can tell you it wasn't pretty."

The editor shifted in his seat, discomfited. "Well," he finally said, "I hate to speak ill of the dead, but Caroline enticed a few of my authors to jump ship to another publisher. I mean, I fully support authors getting the best deal possible and working with the team that suits them best. But it was the way she did it." A frown creased his brow. "Underhanded, to say the least."

"That's unfortunate," Carol said, sending a significant glance toward Molly and Laura. "A lot of people must have resented her."

Joe gave an uncomfortable laugh. "Well, I wouldn't say a lot, but I suppose someone must have." He sighed deeply. "Last time I talked to her—make that the second to last time—she was trying to drum up interest among us editors. She had something big, she said. A real breakout book."

Molly put two and two together. "Was the author named Isla Tod?"

Joe shrugged. "Caroline didn't give a name. She only dropped hints, like bread crumbs, hoping we'd take the bait."

The mysterious Isla Tod. They were no closer to finding her than before. Molly thought of something else. "You said the second to last time you spoke to her. What happened the very last time?" She had a feeling it had been the encounter in Caroline's suite. The room attendant had overheard a heated discussion between Caroline, Joe, and Alyssa.

Joe gave that nervous chuckle again. "Remember what I said about Caroline poaching authors? Alyssa and I were having a little chat with her about that. Some of mine went to Alyssa, but recently

Caroline heavily suggested one of Alyssa's top writers move to yet another publisher." He rubbed his fingers together. "It was all about the money for Caroline. Part of me doesn't blame her. Agents live off commissions, after all. But burning bridges is never a good idea. At the end of the day, publishing is a very small industry."

Molly wondered how deep Joe's resentment toward Caroline went. He had good reason to be angry if the agent had lured moneymaking authors away to a new press. But she could say the same for Alyssa, who was also angry with Gregory—and in the vicinity when both deaths occurred.

"Did you know Gregory?" Molly asked. "He seemed to be such a popular model."

Regret crossed Joe's face. "He was. And a great guy to boot. Our production team hired him for some covers, but not as often as Tartan and Lace. He was on all the Madelaine Alt covers. In fact, we considered that a disadvantage of working with him. He was associated with her titles."

"So a reader might think a book was an Alt title if they saw him, you mean?" Carol asked. "That's like a television actor always associated with one part, even though they try to move on."

"That's a good analogy," Joe said. "We have to balance having a top model on a cover with creating a distinctive brand for our authors."

Patsy Mae was hanging on Joe's every word. "A distinctive brand. I like the sound of that."

Joe smiled at his new author. "I'm glad, because my marketing wheels are already turning. This one book is just the beginning."

Patsy Mae appeared near swooning. "This is such music to my ears, Joe. I can't tell you. I've worked so long and so hard."

Molly was enjoying this glimpse inside the inner world of publishing. Once Patsy Mae's books were on the shelf, she'd be able to say, "I knew her when." Hopefully the editor wasn't involved in Caroline's death. That news would certainly be a crushing blow to her friend.

Kilt-clad men milled about on the lawn, a signal that the sword fighting demonstration would soon begin. Molly noted the heavy swords they were carrying in their belts. "Those aren't what people use for fencing, are they?" she asked the table at large.

Patsy Mae answered, "No, those are Scottish basket-hilted broadswords, the type authentically used in battle. They're much heavier than rapiers."

"They're not sharp, right?" Molly asked. Fergus was supposed to take part, and she didn't want to worry about him getting injured.

"No, of course not," Joe said. "This will be more a demonstration of skill and athletic ability."

Bridget had returned to the table and was sitting in Joyce's seat. "I can't wait to see this event." She put a hand to her chest. "Sword fights are so romantic."

"Too true," Patsy Mae said. "I always include at least one in my books." She pulled her phone out of her bag. "I'm going to film this for future reference. Writing action scenes isn't that easy sometimes."

Molly didn't see Fergus among the men milling about and wondered if he was still going to participate. Then she spotted him walk onto the patio with Deputy Chief Gillespie.

"Excuse me," she said, quickly standing up. Leaving Angus with Carol, she wound her way through the tables and groups of guests to Fergus's side.

"Hi," he said with a smile, noticing her. "I'll be with you in a moment."

Molly stood a slight distance away to allow the two men privacy. After Gillespie left, she moved closer to Fergus.

"Why don't we talk inside?" he suggested, opening the French door for her. "It's a little quieter."

Since the crowd was now cheering raucously for the swordsmen, she laughed. "Make that much quieter."

He closed the door with a click, then faced her, his expression tense in the room's dim lighting. "We didn't find him. Or any trace of him."

Molly's shoulders sagged in relief, releasing tension she didn't even know she was holding. In the back of her mind, she'd been imagining Reg Tod lying in wait for his next hapless victim. "Maybe he's gone. Maybe he was never here." She noticed that Fergus still seemed grim and her heart lurched. "Is there something else?"

"Not a big thing," he said. "But it's odd. We checked Gregory and Caroline's rooms as you suggested. And remember that manuscript by Isla Tod? It's gone."

"The police didn't take it?" Molly had no idea why they would, but they probably removed whatever evidence they found from Caroline's room.

"They said they didn't." Fergus lifted one shoulder in a shrug. "I don't think they believe that a clue to Caroline's death would lie in books written by others. They did take her laptop and a file of correspondence."

"How strange." Molly mulled over this twist. Who would take that manuscript, and why? Maybe this gave greater credence to the theory that Reg was related to Isla—or perhaps using Isla as a pen name. "I suppose it's useless to ask, but did they give you any updates on either case?"

Fergus's expression was rueful. "I'm afraid not. The only new information I have is that Caroline's hair dye was definitely tampered with. The lab narrowed down the ingredient."

Chief Thomson entered the room. "We're going to station a second officer here for the evening," he told Fergus. "If you see or hear anything suspicious, call my cell."

"I'll do that, Chief," Fergus said. "And thank you. It's a great feeling to have such a responsive police force."

Chief Thomson smiled at the genuine compliment, but then his expression sobered. "We're committed to doing a good job for our people." His gaze shifted to Molly. "The same goes for you, Molly, or your friends. You spot anything out of place, call us immediately."

"I will, Chief. Promise." Were Joe's revelations in that category? Molly decided that they might be. "Actually, there is something I want to share. Both editors who visited Caroline before she died had serious issues with her. She was diverting their authors to different publishing houses. And not in a professional way."

The chief didn't respond right away, but Molly could tell he was thinking this information over. "Thank you for sharing that. We'll certainly ask Mr. Byers and Ms. Martin about it should we need to."

To Molly, that indicated that neither editor was being seriously considered as a suspect. She was glad about Joe—unless this was an oversight by the police. Of course, Joe hadn't acted suspiciously the way Reg had. Reg had quit his job the day Caroline died, after he worked in her suite, which was a huge red flag.

Once the chief took his leave, Molly asked Fergus, "Are you still going to be part of the sword fighting?"

Fergus moved to the French door and peered outside. "I was thinking of dropping out, but maybe I should do it. It might burn off a little of my angst." He reached for the door handle. "Coming?"

The event had already begun, with two pairs of fighters squaring off and clashing swords. Molly gathered that the winners would qualify for a later round. Fergus went over to Neil, who was helping organize, while Molly returned to her friends.

Since the competitors couldn't get hurt—although one man fell over dramatically while walking backward—Molly found she enjoyed the spectacle. The men were both strong and graceful, with strategy as important to winning as strength.

"Now I believe that a lot of these guys are in movies," Laura said. "They're obviously trained." As if to underscore her words, one man did a backward flip to evade his opponent and landed on his feet. The crowd clapped and cheered wildly.

Molly didn't think Fergus was an acrobat, so she was extra curious when his turn to fight came up. He kept both feet on the ground, but he was deft, skilled, and ruthless.

"Wow. Fergus is amazing," Laura whispered in her ear.

"He is," Molly said, noticing that her heart was beating a little faster. Even now, in this modern age, women including her were impressed by a man's physical prowess. No wonder historical romance novels sold so well. There weren't many opportunities in ordinary life for men to show off in this way.

Fergus won his match against one of the models, then moved to the sidelines to wait for the next set. In the end, he was one of the winners. Molly ran up to him after he had accepted his trophy. "Fergus, that was amazing." Molly gave him a quick hug. "I had no idea you were such an expert swordsman."

"Me neither," Fergus said with a laugh. "I guess having a lot on your mind helps."

"You were something fierce, mate," one of the other men said. "And here you've got a decade or two on us."

Fergus laughed again. "That's my secret weapon. Everyone underestimates me."

"I don't." Molly smiled up at him. "Want to walk me to my car? Angus and I need to get home." The dog, who was standing at her feet, whined, drawing Fergus's attention.

"You're a good boy," he said, hunkering down to pat Angus, who licked his hand. "I hope you had a good time tonight." The response was a cheerful yip that made both Molly and Fergus laugh.

Molly said goodbye to the others, and she and Fergus walked out to the parking lot. It was fully dark now, a soft, warm summer evening with a light breeze. Stars freckled the inky sky and a quarter moon rode the horizon.

"Where did you park?" Fergus asked as they crossed the pavement. The lot was beginning to empty now since the main event had ended.

Molly pointed. "Over there, at the back."

The route took them past the rear of a huge SUV. As they skirted the vehicle, Molly saw something in the shadows. Angus realized what it was before she did and began to bark. A man lay facedown on the ground.

15

Suddenly breathless, Molly gasped for air. Had someone else been murdered tonight, right under the noses of two police officers? Angus pulled and leaped, trying to get closer, but Molly tugged him backward.

Fergus ran to the man's side and bent down to check his pulse. "It's Joe Byers," he called.

Molly felt herself go pale. Had Joe known something about the murders? Or seen or heard something he shouldn't? And was he—

Before Molly's thoughts went to the worst possible scenario, Fergus called, "He's alive. It looks like someone hit him on the head." His keen gaze surveyed the man's body. "And stole his kilt. Left him his shorts, at least."

Molly frowned. Why would someone steal a kilt?

"Please send an ambulance to Castleglen," Fergus told the dispatcher. "I've got an unconscious man with what appears to be a head injury. Let them know there are two officers already here on-site."

Running footsteps echoed across the parking lot. Deputy Chief Gillespie was first to arrive. He bit back an exclamation when he saw the prone man. "What happened here?"

"That's what I'd like to know," Fergus said, his tone grim. "Someone attacked Joe Byers, one of the editors at the conference, and took his kilt. We won't know if anything else was stolen, like his wallet, until he wakes up."

To Molly's intense relief, she heard a deep groan come from Joe.

"Lie still," Fergus told the man gently. "We've got an ambulance coming."

"What happened?" Joe asked. "Why am I lying on the ground?"

"We think someone attacked you. Your kilt is missing," Fergus said.

Gillespie asked, "Do you remember anything? Anything at all?"

"I'm afraid not," Joe said. "Last thing I knew, I was walking to my rental car. I needed something from the trunk."

Flashing lights appeared in the distance, headed their way down the winding entry road. The ambulance had arrived.

"I'll go meet them," Gillespie said, starting off across the parking lot.

Officer Michael Drummond, also dressed in street clothes, came running up to Gillespie. "Sorry it took me so long," he said. "I was at the other end of the property."

"No problem," Gillespie said. He waved at the driver of the ambulance and pointed, indicating the direction they should go. The bulky vehicle slowed and eased between the rows of parked cars.

The EMTs parked, opened the rear doors of the ambulance, and got to work. "All his vitals are good," one told the officers and Fergus. "But we're taking him to the medical center to make sure he doesn't have a concussion."

"Good idea," Fergus said. "Head injuries can be tricky."

As the EMTs lifted Joe onto a gurney, the deputy chief turned to Drummond. "Why don't you tag along? Take a statement when he's fit for it. See if he remembers anything from before he was hit."

"Sure thing," Drummond said. "I'll go right down." He paused. "Are you going to search the grounds again?"

Gillespie sighed. "We'd better. Although if our man has any brains, he'll be holed up somewhere we won't find him."

Judging by the way Reg Tod had eluded capture so far, Molly thought lack of brains wasn't an issue. He always seemed to stay one step ahead of the police.

"Did you hear the news?" Carol asked as Molly entered the bakehouse kitchen the next morning. "There's still a BOLO out on Reg Tod's whereabouts."

"Did they say he was kilted and dangerous?" Molly quipped as she headed for the coffee. "I was hoping they would find him last night." She paused to suppress a yawn. "If it *was* him who stole Joe's kilt, that is."

Laura snorted a laugh as she leafed through her recipe book. "I'm sorry. I know it's awful, but it's also absurd. Who on earth would take someone's kilt?"

Carol used a spatula to remove parlies, Scottish biscuits similar to gingersnaps, from a tray. "Someone who wants to blend in with other people. He's tall, and like I said before, almost handsome. At a glance, people at the conference will probably think he's a cover model."

Molly reveled in her first sip of delicious coffee. "That's what I thought too. He's awfully brave to show his face around Castleglen, though. Everyone is searching for him, kilt or not."

"I don't get it," Laura said. "Why is he still hanging around? And why did he run off? He doesn't seem to have any connection to either of the victims. He's a handyman from Harvey, Michigan."

Molly grabbed a second spatula to work on a tray of cookies. "Speaking of which, did you hear back from your parents?"

Laura nodded. "I did, but unfortunately they don't remember the Tods. They must have moved to town after we left."

Carol picked up the tray of cookies and walked toward the kitchen door. "Isn't Harvey near Marquette?"

"Yes," Laura said. "A few miles south of the city. I haven't been there since . . . I can't remember when."

Carol halted with her back against the swinging kitchen door. "How would you two feel about a road trip this afternoon? Maybe we can learn more about the mysterious Reginald Tod if we go to Harvey."

"I'm game," Molly agreed. Bridget and Hamish were both coming in to work this afternoon and could handle the customers and closing tasks. Molly had planned to go to a class at the conference, but it wasn't something she minded missing.

"Sounds like a plan," Laura said with a smile. "It will be kind of fun to return to my old stomping grounds."

Molly's cell phone rang and Patsy Mae's name appeared on the display. She took off her glove and answered it. "Good morning, Patsy Mae," she greeted her friend. "How are you?"

"I'm awful," Patsy Mae declared. "I didn't sleep a wink. I kept imagining that Reg Tod was breaking into my room."

As far as Molly knew, Reg had no possible reason to do that, but she didn't say so. Instead, she tried to reassure Patsy Mae. "I'm sure they'll find him soon," she said. "Loch Mallaig isn't that big."

"I hope so." Patsy Mae sighed. "My nerves can't take this. And poor Joe. Thankfully his head is okay, but I'm sure he can't wait for this conference to be over."

"Tomorrow night is the ball," Molly said. "That's the last big event aside from the closing breakfast."

"If we all live that long," Patsy Mae said wryly, then paused. "So, I hope you ladies don't mind . . ."

"What is it?" Molly asked.

"That nice writer, Linda, and her friends invited me to a brainstorming session. Those tend to last a while, so I'll be a bit tied up," Patsy Mae said in a rush, clearly worried she might be offending the Bakehouse Three by accepting an offer to spend time with others. "I figure, safety in numbers."

Molly smiled, glad Patsy Mae was making new friends. "That's wonderful. Laura, Carol, and I have to go out of town this afternoon anyway, but we'll be back tonight." Molly was tempted to tell Patsy Mae what they were doing but she thought it better to be discreet. While she trusted Patsy Mae, she also knew it was easy to let things slip.

"I'll see you tonight, then," Patsy Mae said, sounding relieved.

"I'll call you later." After Molly disconnected, she said, "Patsy Mae's nerves are fraying. I really, really hope this ordeal is over soon."

"Me too," Laura said. "I just had to read the same recipe twice, I'm so distracted."

Carol returned to the kitchen and heard this last. She was eating one of the fresh parlies. "But your baking skills are intact, I'm happy to report." She waved the cookie and grinned. "This one broke so I had to eat it."

Instead of leaving Angus at home alone during their road trip, Molly agreed readily when Harvey offered to come get him. He arrived at the bakehouse early that afternoon when they were getting ready to leave.

"Thank you so much," Molly said. "He gets lonely when I'm gone."

"Wouldn't want that," Harvey said. He smiled down at Angus. "Us boys are going to have a good time." Angus jumped up and put his paws on Harvey's leg, his tail wagging.

"He obviously thinks so too," Molly said. She handed Harvey a bag containing Angus's dinner and treats before opening the rear door of Carol's Chrysler. "See you both later."

"I'll text you when we're on the way home." Carol gave her husband a kiss. "Don't worry about dinner. We'll grab something on the road."

Harvey guided Angus toward his Jeep. "Have a good trip, ladies. See you when you get back."

Carol got into the driver's side and Laura, who was most familiar with their destination, took the front passenger seat so she could navigate. Molly set a tote containing a thermos of coffee, cups, cookies, and bottles of water on the rear seat beside her, then buckled her seat belt.

Soon they were leaving Loch Mallaig, driving toward Marquette. The route led them along Lake Superior, providing gorgeous vistas of the lake and surrounding countryside. Molly sat back and tried to relax, knowing that she couldn't do much of anything until they reached their destination. She did send Fergus a text to let him know she was out of town, but she didn't say why. If they learned anything interesting, of course she would share it—with Fergus and the police.

She certainly hoped they would unravel the mystery of Reg Tod, at least a little. How was he connected to the victims? Or *was* he? Maybe it was simply a case of wrong place, wrong time for the poor man. He might have run away because he believed he was being framed or would otherwise be blamed.

But then why linger? If Molly had been in his shoes, she would have left the state at least. With his skills, he could pick up a job anywhere or, better yet, do casual labor for cash.

Molly laughed to herself. So much for relaxing. With an effort, she put aside her circular thoughts about Reg and the murders and focused on the view. Sailboats dotted the massive lake, and she tried to imagine what it was like out there, so far from shore and the troubles of daily life. Nothing but wind and water and sky.

The town of Harvey was on the other side of Marquette, more of a suburb than a separate town, Laura informed them. As they drove along Harvey's main drag, Molly spotted a typical array of businesses interspersed with houses and undeveloped land. There was a definite rural feel to the place despite its proximity to the small city of Marquette.

"It hasn't changed much," Laura said. "Want to see where we used to live?"

"Sure," Carol said, her hand moving to the dashboard GPS. "What's the address?" Laura gave it to her and she punched it in. Then Carol glanced at Molly in the rearview mirror. "Did you happen to find the Tods' address?"

"Yes," Molly said. "I searched the deed records for his parents and got an address. There isn't any record of sale from Reg or his parents, so I bet he still owns the property." She rattled off the address.

"Guess what?" Laura said. "That's very close to our old house. Two birds with one stone."

"How efficient of us," Carol said with a laugh, signaling a turn off the main road.

They entered a neighborhood of modest homes—a mix of ranches, bungalows, and newer houses. Laura's former home was a cute ranch with a neat patch of yard.

"I remember it so well," Laura said. "I loved it, but it wasn't quite big enough for us as Brody and I got older. Imagine sharing a bedroom with your *gross* older brother." Everyone laughed at her dramatic delivery.

Molly saw a swing set and sandbox in the backyard. "Looks like a family lives there. How sweet."

"We used to have a swing set too," Laura said. "But it was metal. I remember the legs thumping up and down when we swung too high. It used to give my mother fits." She rolled down the car window and snapped a few photographs.

"We did the same thing," Molly said, remembering her own childhood.

They gazed at Laura's old home for a few more minutes while she shared memories, then mutually decided it was time to continue with their mission.

As Laura had said, Reg's home was a few streets away in the same neighborhood. Carol slowed as they approached the 1950s ranch, which was similar to Laura's. The house appeared to be in decent shape, but the grass was overgrown and dead leaves lay scattered on the path and porch. The windows were dark, giving the place a forlorn and neglected feel.

Carol rolled to a stop in front. "It doesn't look like he's home."

"No surprise," Molly said. "I'm sure the police have been coming by on a regular basis to see if he's here. He's probably too smart to return to a known address."

An older woman emerged from the house next door, pulling on a pair of gardening gloves as she carefully crossed her porch. Her eyes still on Carol's car, she descended the porch steps and moved toward a flower bed full of tulips. She carefully knelt down and began to weed.

"Why don't we go talk to her?" Molly said, reaching for the door handle. "Before she calls the police on us."

The noise of the car doors opening and closing caused the woman to rise to her feet. She stood with both hands at her side, a concerned expression on her face. "Can I help you?" she called.

"I hope so." Molly took the lead, making sure to smile in what she hoped was an encouraging manner. "We came to see Reg Tod, but he's not home."

The woman folded her arms, immediately skeptical. "Of course he's not. He's wanted by the police." She cocked a brow. "Are you from the press? There's been a constant stream of you people ever since the BOLO went out."

Molly laughed. "No we're not. Honest. We actually live in Loch

Mallaig, where Reg was working. We own a bakehouse there." Molly gave her name, then introduced Laura and Carol.

The woman's stance relaxed. "Nice to meet you. I'm Sadie Weston." She gestured to the front porch, where several wicker chairs sat. "Would you like a cup of coffee or something cold to drink?"

The three women agreed that a cup of coffee would be wonderful, and settled on the porch while Sadie went inside.

"I'm a little surprised she's being so welcoming," Carol murmured, clearly aware that only a screen door separated them from Sadie.

"She's probably curious," Laura said quietly. "I know I would be if my neighbor was involved in a couple of homicides."

A few minutes later, Sadie bustled through the screen door carrying a tray with four mugs, a sugar bowl, and a pitcher of milk, plus napkins and spoons. She set the tray on a low table. "Help yourself. We don't stand on ceremony around here."

Everyone reached for a mug and doctored the coffee to their preferences.

A sly smile crept across Sadie's face. "While I was inside, I did a search for you on the Internet." She lifted her mug and took a sip. "I love the name of your business. Bread on Arrival. So clever."

How smart of Sadie, Molly reflected, to not take their word for it. "Our building used to be a funeral home," she explained. "So the name was a natural fit."

Carol, ever prepared, pulled a glossy advertising card out of her handbag. "If you're ever in Loch Mallaig, please come by. We'd love to see you again."

Sadie studied the card, lips pursed. "Isn't that kind of you?" She put the card down. "So tell me, what's been going on up there? You can't really trust the news to get things right."

Molly gave a brief recap, with Laura and Carol chiming in. "We're really concerned about our friend," Molly concluded. "She happened to be there when both murders were discovered."

"And so did Molly," Laura pointed out.

Sadie gasped. "You poor thing. What a shock that must have been."

"It was," Molly admitted. "Anyway, we can't help but feel that Reg must know something important. I'm not totally convinced that he's guilty, although running off certainly made him look it."

Sadie issued an indelicate huff. "He's not guilty. Reg Tod wouldn't hurt a fly. My grandkids call him the gentle giant, because he's so tall. He's helped me out more times than I can count, whenever I need a hand or something repaired around here. Reg is good that way."

"He's a talented repairman by all accounts," Molly said. "His employer at Castleglen really valued him. That's why he was so shocked when Reg ran off." She'd decided not to mention the possibility that Reg was still lurking around the resort. Sadie was a nice woman, but in all likelihood she'd share that tidbit, possibly with the press. All the police—or Fergus—needed was a news article saying that Reg was still at Castleglen.

Sadie had chosen a rocker and now she rocked back and forth a few times. "No, I can't see Reg as a killer. I've known him ever since he was a small boy, when he and his family moved in next door. He and his brother used to play with my kids all the time."

Molly's eyebrows shot up. "I didn't realize Reg had a brother."

"Twins," Sadie said. "Reg and Roger. Isn't that cute?"

Molly's mind immediately flashed to the room attendant, Paula, mentioning how similar Reg and Gregory were. "Were they identical?" she asked. If the answer was yes, that would shoot down her theory before she could fully form it.

"No, fraternal." Sadie chuckled. "Roger got the better end of the deal, to be frank. He was so handsome, he could have been a model."

16

Only the creak of Sadie's rocker broke the silence that fell over the Bakehouse Three. Molly saw her confused thoughts reflected in the wide-eyed expressions on Laura and Carol's faces.

"Roger was the dominant twin, as sometimes happens," Sadie continued. "And it was more than just their appearances. He was the more outgoing and sociable one of the two. The leader, if you will."

Carol cleared her throat. "Where is Roger now?"

Molly held her breath waiting for the answer, knowing that once again, her wild supposition could collapse in an instant.

Distress etched Sadie's soft features. "It's such a sad story. Roger and his family were estranged. I never knew exactly what happened, just his parents disapproved of how he wanted to live his life, and Reg sided with his mom and dad. I haven't seen Roger for twenty-two years, since he turned eighteen."

Molly thought about asking Sadie if she had any pictures of Roger, but dismissed that as too hard to explain. She certainly didn't want to raise the idea of Roger moving to Scotland, changing his name to Gregory Gregg, and becoming a famous cover model.

"I'm so sorry to hear that," Molly said. "I take it he didn't come to his parents' funerals?"

"No, I'm afraid not," Sadie said. "We were all keeping an eye out for him. You'd think that would bring him back if anything would."

"Poor Reg," Laura said. "All alone now. How was he doing?"

What a great question, Molly thought. Reg's state of mind

might well be a huge factor in this case, the reason he went to Loch Mallaig in the first place. If Gregory was indeed his long-lost brother, Roger.

Sadie pressed her lips together. "Not too well. He lived in Detroit for a while before his folks died, but he moved back to take care of them when they got sick. Since they died, he's been spending most of the past few months holed up in his house. Oh, he'd leave to go to his jobs or to get groceries. Still, I was starting to get worried about him. I thought he might be clinically depressed."

Or homicidal. "Hopefully they will locate him soon," Molly said. "And if he is depressed, get him the treatment he needs."

"I hope so," Sadie said. "We miss him around here. The old Reg, that is."

A short while later, the Bakehouse Three took their leave of Sadie, with profuse thanks for the nice break and with hopes that she would visit them in Loch Mallaig.

"Any ideas where to go next?" Molly asked as they drove away, returning Sadie's wave as she went back to weeding her tulip bed.

"Harvey doesn't have its own high school," Laura said. "And I want to get a peek at Reg and Roger's yearbook. I say we hit the library."

"Great idea," Molly said. "Libraries often collect local yearbooks."

The closest branch, in central Marquette, was a gorgeous stone building in the classical style. As they climbed the wide front steps, Molly felt her heart lift with anticipation. She loved libraries. They promised entry to whole new worlds of learning and imagination.

The reference area was located on the upper level, and thanks to the assistance of a kind librarian, they soon located the shelf of yearbooks.

"I wonder what year they graduated," Laura said, hunkering down to study the spines. "Sadie said the last time she saw Gregory was twenty-two years ago."

"Grab that year and the ones on on either side," Carol suggested. "Sometimes people graduate early or late, depending on their birthdays."

Laura selected three books and carried them over to a nearby table, then slid one each to Molly and Carol. Working in silence, they paged through the glossy annuals.

Rather than flip right to the "Ts" in the senior section, Molly leafed through each page. All those bright young faces, so hopeful and excited. She wondered where they were now. How different from her own yearbook too, which had featured posed formal shots. In this one, the teens had chosen their own settings, including outside and full-body photographs rather than headshots. So much more relaxed.

Carol closed her book with a light thud. "Nothing?" Laura asked. Carol shook her head.

Molly went through the alphabet a little faster and found the right page. And here was Roger Tod. Even two decades later, his face was unmistakable. He was now known to the world as Gregory Gregg.

Excitement bubbled in her chest as she turned the book so the others could see. "It's him," she whispered. "Look." Roger was lounging in a doorway, his handsome, serious face set off by the black-and-white photo. In contrast, Reg leaned against the bumper of an old pickup truck, wearing a friendly, gap-toothed grin.

Carol tapped the page with her forefinger. "That's him, all right. Do you think Reg knew famous model Gregory Gregg was his brother?"

"He must have," Laura said. "Why else would he go to Loch Mallaig right before the convention?"

Laura's words hung in the air. Molly dug for her phone and snapped pictures of the brothers. "I want to show these to Fergus when we get back."

"I wonder if the police have put this together yet," Carol said thoughtfully. "They must have, while digging into Reg's background. Right?"

"That's probably why they're convinced he's a killer," Molly said. "But they're keeping this under wraps, which means we should as well." She paused. "Well, except for Fergus, naturally."

"I get it," Carol said. "I tell Harvey everything. That's why we have such a good marriage."

Molly stilled at Carol's reference to marriage. Was Fergus more than a good friend? She examined her feelings for a moment and came to a conclusion—a big, fat *maybe*. He was certainly an important part of her life, no doubt about that.

Molly's phone bleeped with a text. "Speak of the devil," she murmured, seeing Fergus's name.

When are you heading home? he asked.

Soon, Molly wrote. *We're going to grab something to eat first.*

Safe travels, he replied, including a cute smiley face. *Let me know when you make it back.*

Such sweet concern. Fergus was her friend all right, and a very good one. Molly tucked her phone away. "What's next?"

"I'd like to know more about the Tods," Laura said. "We still don't know if the twins are connected to Isla Tod, whoever she is."

"Good point," Molly said. "It might be a coincidence that someone picked that last name, but somehow I doubt it."

A nearby computer held digitized editions of the local newspaper, fortunately easily searchable.

Laura took the lead. She sat on the desk chair and typed in *Reginald Tod*. That brought up the obituaries for his parents, with no mention of Roger. "No Isla here," Laura said.

"Try searching for their father's name," Carol suggested. "Maybe Isla is from an older generation in his family."

The keys clicked as Laura entered the information. Results loaded and she opened the top one. "Bingo," she said. "The twins' great-grandmother was named Isla Tod. I'll bet one of them used it as a pen name."

"Could be, but I'm not sure that means anything," Carol said.

"True," Molly said, her excitement deflating. "We don't know for sure if the manuscript is connected to the murders."

Laura whirled around in the chair, which had a spinning seat. "But we don't know that it doesn't, either." She patted her midriff. "Who's ready for dinner? I'm starving."

They were eating fish and chips at a local seafood restaurant when Molly noticed that she had a voice mail. "I didn't even hear my phone ring," she remarked, picking up her phone to listen to her messages.

"It must have come in while we were in a dead zone," Carol said. She checked at her own phone. "I had a missed call too, but I don't recognize the number."

"Same here." Laura grimaced. "I hope there isn't an emergency."

The bakehouse was closed, so the call couldn't have been from Bridget or Hamish with a question or issue. Besides, all three of them had their employees' numbers in their phones. The message was from Patsy Mae, as it turned out. "Hi Molly, I hope you're having a good day. I just wanted to let you know that I've decided to leave the conference early. It was great seeing you all. Say bye to the others for me."

"Listen to this," Molly said, playing the message so Carol and Laura could hear. "I wish she hadn't left while we were out of town." Disappointment knotted in her chest. She was going to miss Patsy Mae.

"Maybe that brainstorming session didn't go well, and she

decided she was done with the conference," Carol said. "I can't say I'd blame her. It's been much more dramatic than she was probably anticipating."

"I hope she doesn't get in trouble with the police," Laura said, her brow creased with concern. "She's a witness in both cases."

"They could have given her permission." Carol dipped a French fry in her puddle of ketchup. "Patsy Mae is way too law-abiding to leave without it."

"There's only one way to find out." Molly dialed Patsy Mae's number, but it rang and rang until voice mail kicked on. "Please call me when you get this, Patsy Mae. We're really sad that you left. It was great seeing you."

"She might be in the air," Carol said as Molly hung up.

Molly nodded. "I'll keep trying until I get her." Picking up her fork, she cut into flaky, fresh fish. "I'd better eat up so we can get on the road."

When they arrived at Carol's house, Harvey and Angus were watching the news. Upon spotting his mistress, Angus jumped down from Harvey's lap and trotted across the floor, nails clicking.

Molly scooped him up. "Did you miss me, boy?" Angus licked her chin in answer.

"I'll put the kettle on," Carol said, then headed to the kitchen with Laura. They'd decided to have a cup of tea before Carol ran Molly and Laura back to the bakehouse.

"We had a good time," Harvey said. He seemed quite comfortable, lounging in his recliner with his slippers on. "We took a long walk by the lake and played with a ball."

"Thanks so much for watching him," Molly said. Her gaze fell on the television, which Harvey had muted. "Can you turn that up, please?"

"Sure." Harvey reached for the remote and complied.

The newscaster said, "Police are still looking for handyman Reginald Tod, wanted for questioning in two deaths." A picture of Reg flashed onto the screen. "An incident last night leads them to believe that the suspect is still in the Loch Mallaig area. If you see this man, please call the police immediately. Do not approach him. Reginald Tod is considered dangerous and may be armed."

"You don't think anything will happen at the ball tomorrow night, do you?" Harvey asked. "It might not be safe."

"You're not trying to get out of wearing white tie and a kilt, are you?" Carol called teasingly from the kitchen.

"Either way, I'm still going," Molly said. "Fergus needs our support. I'm worried about his business being damaged in all of this."

Harvey rubbed his chin. "Good point. Well, I suppose we'll be safe enough. As Carol said before, Reg Tod isn't interested in us."

"We learned something today that shines a different light on things," Molly said. "Reg is, or was, Gregory Gregg's twin brother."

Harvey's brows rose. "Are you serious? Wow. So he did have a reason to be at the resort. He wanted to see his brother."

Or kill him. Molly's belly squirmed, much the way Angus was wiggling in her arms. She set him gently on the floor, and he ran back to Harvey and jumped up into his lap again. The kettle whistled, followed by the thump of cupboard doors closing.

Molly perched on an armchair. "There's more, but I'll wait until Carol and Laura sit down."

"You'll wait for us why?" Carol laughed as she carried a tray into the living room, Laura behind her.

"Oh, I started spilling all the beans about Reg," Molly said. She took the basket of tea bags Carol handed her and leafed through, settling on a calming herbal blend.

After everyone had their tea, the trio filled Harvey in on the results of their trip to Harvey and Marquette.

"You amaze me." Harvey beamed proudly. "No one can keep secrets from you three."

Carol smiled at her husband. "High praise from a former investigative journalist."

"I could have used your talents a time or two," Harvey said.

They chatted for a while, discussing plans for the next day. After a full day at the bakehouse, they would all be attending the ball, the conference's capstone event.

"I wonder what Chief Thomson will do if they don't solve the case before tomorrow night," Molly said. "All the conference guests will want to go home."

"Actually, I'm surprised any are still here," Carol said. "I wonder if some of them took off like Patsy Mae."

"Maybe so. And that reminds me." Molly sent Patsy Mae a text. Hopefully she was either back in Louisiana or between flights. She'd feel better once she talked to her friend. But her phone remained stubbornly silent.

"I hope she doesn't forget about us now that she's left Loch Mallaig," Carol said. "It happens so often with old friends. You're happy to see them but once they go home, you lose touch again."

Another possibility might be that Patsy Mae was traumatized by her experience here and would avoid all reminders. Molly devoutly hoped that wasn't the case.

Laura glanced at the time. "I hate to say it, but we'd better get going. I'll be up bright and early tomorrow to bake."

"Good thing you're all morning people," Harvey said, settling into his recliner.

Molly stood with a laugh and a stretch. "We would have had to find a different business idea if we weren't."

Carol got to her feet with a groan. "Let me run you down." She picked up the empty mugs and placed them on the tray.

"Don't worry about that," Harvey said. "I'll load them into the dishwasher. We've almost got a full load."

"You're a peach, Harvey MacCallan," Laura said, draining the rest of her tea.

As they were driving toward town, Molly's phone rang. She didn't recognize the number but she answered anyway. "Hello?"

"Hi, is this Molly Ferris?" The caller was a young woman who sounded like she was about Chloe's age.

"It is," Molly said. "How can I help you?"

"This is Lauren, Patsy Mae's daughter. I haven't heard from her." The caller inhaled audibly, and her next words were shaky. "I'm getting very worried."

17

A chill hit Molly's core. Where was Patsy Mae? And why was she out of touch with her family? "All I know is this," she said, trying to keep her voice level so she wouldn't scare Lauren. "Your mom left me a message saying she was leaving the conference. I was out of town and I didn't hear the phone ringing, unfortunately." If only Molly had spoken to Patsy Mae. She would have gotten more details about what exactly her friend was planning.

Lauren gave a sob of distress. "I've tried calling the airlines and the car rental place, but they won't tell me anything. I'm so worried."

So was Molly, but she couldn't let it show. She had to be strong, like she would want her friends to be for Chloe. "Lauren, I'm going to go by the resort where she was staying and speak to the owner. Maybe they know something. And if they don't, we'll talk to the police."

"It's not like Mom to do this. She always texts me when she gets on a plane and when she lands." Lauren was outright crying now. "Even when she turns in for the night. She sent me regular messages while she was at the conference."

"We'll do our best to locate her or find out where she went," Molly said. "Stand by. I'll call you back shortly."

Carol and Laura had of course been listening in. "One of Patsy Mae's kids?" Carol asked after Molly had hung up.

"Yes, her daughter. She hasn't heard from Patsy Mae either, and she's very concerned." Molly dialed Fergus's cell phone.

To her relief, Fergus answered right away. "Molly, what's up?"

"I'm sorry to bother you," Molly said, "but it appears that Patsy Mae may have gone missing."

"Gone missing?" His tone was immediately alert. "What do you mean?"

Molly relayed the sequence of events. "We're going right by the resort. Is there any chance that you're still there?" Questioning the staff would be easier with the owner present.

"I sure am," Fergus said. "I was just about to head out, but I'll wait. Where are you?"

Glancing out the window, she recognized their location. "We'll be there in five minutes. We went to Harvey, Michigan, today. And we learned something very interesting. I'll tell you when we get there."

"You know how to torture a man," Fergus said. "I'll meet you in the lobby."

Carol pulled into a space by the door. "I'll move if someone needs it," she said.

"Nice offer, but I doubt you'll have to," Laura said, opening her car door. "People don't usually check in this late."

"And hopefully we won't be here long." Molly couldn't wait to go to bed, where hopefully she would sleep.

Fergus was standing by the front desk when they entered. He waved them over. "While I was waiting, we checked the system. Patsy Mae did check out."

"I came on at four," the young clerk said. "So I wasn't here, unfortunately. But that's what the system says." She clicked computer keys. "No one is in there if you'd like to take a peek."

There was probably nothing to see, but Molly said, "We might as well. Maybe there's a clue to her travel arrangements."

The clerk continued to tap keys. "We had her vehicle information, but it's doubtful that the rental company will tell you anything." Her smile was crooked. "I've tried."

"Maybe they won't tell us," Carol said. "But I bet they'll tell the police." At the clerk's gasp, she added, "Not that we think anything happened to Patsy Mae. We're checking on her at the request of her daughter."

Fergus headed for the elevator, and they all followed. Up on the third floor, the corridor was hushed, with many guests still at dinner or attending an evening conference event.

"The sword fighting event was great fun," Carol said. "Congratulations on doing so well, Fergus."

"Thanks." Fergus gripped his shoulder with a grimace. "I'm feeling it today, I tell you." He opened the door with a master key.

It was obvious at first glance that the room hadn't been cleaned yet, and Molly was glad. As they drifted inside, she went right for the trash can, thinking of something she always did when traveling. A brief forage through the bag and she was successful. "Here it is. The baggage tag from Patsy Mae's suitcase." The tag revealed which airline she had traveled on to the conference.

"Good work, Molly," Fergus said.

Molly offered a wry smile. "I always rip off the old one before I leave for the airport. And usually not until then."

Carol and Laura were busy searching the bathroom. "Found something," Carol said, waving a brochure as she emerged back to the main room. "This is for a car rental company."

"And I found this," Laura said, holding up a state map with a route marked out to Loch Mallaig. It was the sort of publication given out in airports.

"That's great," Molly said. "At least we have something to give the police." Otherwise, searching for Patsy Mae would be like searching a haystack for a needle.

"And speaking of which," Fergus said. "I'm going to give Chief Thomson a call."

They hovered in the room while Fergus phoned the chief and explained the situation. He also passed along what they'd gleaned about Patsy Mae's movements. Fergus then listened for a couple of minutes, occasionally murmuring assent, before hanging up.

"What did he say?" Laura asked. "Are they going to look for her?"

Fergus shook his head. "Not yet. She's an adult who left the resort voluntarily. The fact that she's been out of touch with friends and family isn't enough. He wants us to give it another day."

Molly plopped down on the end of the bed. "Maybe she's still in transit. Or her phone is dead." There was no reason to panic yet, right?

"Did he have any other updates?" Carol asked. "Have the police located Reg Tod yet?"

Fergus slid his phone into his pocket. "Not yet. They got a hot tip that he was seen out near Ironwood, so they're focused on that area now."

"Ironwood? That's over a hundred miles away." Laura's expression was skeptical. "Why would he go there?"

"Apparently he has family out that way," Fergus said.

Molly snapped her fingers as the mention of Reg's family brought the information about his twin to mind. "Oh Fergus, I was going to tell you what we learned today. Reg had a twin named Roger, but we're pretty sure he was actually Gregory Gregg."

"In fact, we're almost positive," Carol said. "The yearbook pictures we saw at the library clinched it."

"You ladies were certainly busy." Fergus shook his head in amazement. "Wow. They were fraternal twins, right? Similar, but not identical."

"And the next door neighbor told us that Gregory—well, Roger—had been estranged from his family for years," Laura added. "He didn't even come to his parents' funerals."

"And he wasn't mentioned in their obituaries either," Carol said. "So the ill will was on both sides."

Fergus rubbed his chin. "I wonder if the police know about this."

Molly glanced at the other two women. "We thought they must, if they were digging into Reg and Roger's backgrounds."

"I think we should mention it to the chief anyway. Never assume, right?" Fergus dug his phone out of his pocket again. "Do you mind if I call him?"

The women agreed, but by the wincing expression on Fergus's face while speaking to Chief Thomson, Molly guessed that he already knew about the relationship between the murdered man and the fugitive—and that he wasn't thrilled with the Bakehouse Three's meddling.

Fergus attempted a smile after he hung up. "The chief was well aware of the situation. After he was done remarking on your . . . investigating talents, he said to say thank you. But he also warned us to keep the connection between Reg and Roger quiet. He doesn't want the media to get hold of it because they will go absolutely wild."

So far it seemed that even old friends like Sadie hadn't realized that Roger Tod was actually Gregory Gregg. But Molly was sure it was only a matter of time before someone put two and two together.

"We won't say anything to anyone," Molly promised. "Let's just hope they find Reg soon. And that Patsy Mae gets in touch."

"There's more," Laura told Fergus. "Remember the manuscript that went missing from Caroline's room? By Isla Tod?"

"Yes I do," Fergus said. "That was really strange, although the police weren't convinced it was related to her death."

"Isla Tod is the name of the twins' great-grandmother," Laura said. "So there must be a connection between them and the book."

"It would seem so," Fergus said. "Next time I talk to the chief, I'll mention it. Hopefully he'll appreciate the news."

Molly picked up her phone. "Before we go, I need to call Lauren back and give her the update."

Lauren of course wanted the police to start looking for her mother right away.

"They want to give it a little time," Molly told her. "There's no sign of foul play. We checked her room, and everything is as it should be."

"Thanks for the information," Lauren said. "I'll try not to panic until tomorrow morning. But if Mom doesn't show up soon, I'm going to call the Loch Mallaig police myself."

"And we'll call you immediately if we hear from her," Molly said. "I promise."

"Any time, even if it's the middle of the night," Lauren urged. "Please."

"Absolutely," Molly said. "We totally understand your concern."

When they walked out the resort entrance doors a few minutes later, Molly sighed. "I can't wait to get home and go to bed."

"Same here," Carol said. "Hop in and I'll drive you both back." Laura had parked at the bakehouse and was going to pick up her car there.

On the way back to town, Molly stared out the car window into the night. She wasn't sure what she was expecting or hoping to see, but she felt as if she had to keep her eyes peeled for Reg Tod and Patsy Mae. She checked her phone for about the millionth time. No missed calls, no new texts. She felt like screaming and could only imagine what Lauren was going through. Hopefully tomorrow would bring good news.

After Carol dropped her off, Molly let Angus out, then gave him fresh water and a bedtime snack. Once she'd changed into her pajamas, she made a cup of hot cocoa with marshmallows. She wasn't quite ready for sleep, so she curled up on the sofa and turned on the television.

The local news was on, and the headline story was the missing Reg Tod. Blurry footage from Ironwood showed the supposed sighting of the man, who was inside a convenience store purchasing chips and a soda. He was tall but wore a ball cap low over his face so his features weren't clearly visible. Other footage showed him outside the store, getting into a sedan parked at the edge of the lot.

A sedan? Molly remembered that Reg drove a truck, so this was probably a false lead. Something about the size and color of the sedan rang a bell, though. Then the picture changed back to the newscaster, who urged anyone who had seen Reg Tod to call the police immediately.

"You bet I would," Molly said to Angus, who was curled up next to her on the sofa. "Are you ready for bed, big guy? I sure am." Tomorrow morning would come all too quickly.

After rolling around for hours, Molly finally fell into a deep slumber. Then of course the alarm went off all too soon, shocking her awake. Opening one eye, she peered at the time, hoping there was some mistake. Unfortunately not. She groaned softly then threw the covers back.

"Up and at 'em," she said to Angus, who was still sleeping. He sat up with a shake of his head and yawned dramatically. "Guess you didn't sleep very well either." She ruffled his fur and stood.

After showering and dressing, Molly took Angus outside. She stood in the backyard, fighting back yawns as the dog frolicked in the grass. At least one of them had snapped out of their stupor.

Laura arrived in her red Beetle convertible. "How are you this morning?" she called as she got out of the car. As usual, she looked bright and fresh.

"Didn't get much sleep," Molly said. "Other than that, we're fine."

"I'll go put the coffee on then." Laura disappeared through the back door.

"Angus, come," Molly called. She needed to put him inside and get to work herself.

Seeing Bridget arrive in the parking lot, Angus abandoned his inspection of a flower bed and bounded across the grass. He waited by the gate, tail wagging like a metronome, for her to come in and pat him.

"Good morning," Molly said. "You're here early."

"I told Laura I could come in and help set up," Bridget said, bending over to give Angus a head rub. "It's been such a busy week."

"And we've been out more than usual. We really appreciate your help, Bridget. We couldn't do it without you."

The young woman's cheeks flushed at the praise. "Or Hamish. He's been here every day too." Giving Angus a final pat, she straightened. "I saw your friend Patsy Mae yesterday."

Molly's heart skipped a beat. "You did? When? And where?"

"I went out to the resort to play a few holes of golf yesterday after work with Neil MacGregor and a couple of friends," Bridget said. "I ran into Patsy Mae walking through the lobby with her suitcase. She said she had checked out. I was surprised because the conference doesn't end until tomorrow morning."

"That's right, the ball is tonight and tomorrow is the final breakfast." Molly gnawed at her lower lip, wondering how much she should tell Bridget. It wasn't a good idea to spread panic, she decided. "Patsy Mae called me yesterday to tell me she was leaving, but it went to voice mail since we were in the middle of nowhere on our way to Marquette."

"I know all about that dead zone," Bridget said, rolling her eyes. She fell into step with Molly as they strolled toward the building. "Patsy Mae seems like such a nice lady. It's too bad you didn't get a chance to say goodbye."

"Yes, we were disappointed about that," Molly said. "Hopefully we'll see her again soon. What time did you guys start your round?"

This was an opportunity to find out when Patsy Mae had left the resort, she realized.

"About five o'clock." Bridget smiled, and Molly thought her expression was almost bashful. "Neil let us play for free since it was so late in the day. He's the best."

"Yes he is," Molly said. *And so is his father.* "See you in a couple of minutes, Bridget. Tell Laura I'll be right down."

As she walked Angus around to the outside stairs, she realized she needed to call Lauren with this update. They had a witness who had seen Patsy Mae leaving the resort late yesterday afternoon—but the clerk had said she'd checked out before four. Maybe Patsy Mae had done more brainstorming with Linda or gone to a workshop or relaxed on the grounds before leaving the resort.

But whatever she had been up to, questions remained. Where was she right now? And why hadn't she contacted anyone?

18

After Bridget's revelation, Molly waited to call Lauren until after seven, thinking even that was too early. But Patsy Mae's daughter answered immediately. "Any news?" she asked without preamble.

"A young woman who works with me saw Patsy Mae leaving the resort at five yesterday afternoon," Molly said. "She had her suitcase and was heading through the lobby toward the parking lot."

Lauren gave a groan of dismay. "I've checked the flight times and there were a couple of late ones she could have taken. But she still hasn't shown up. And her phone keeps going right to voice mail."

"Did you try contacting the rental car company again? Did they tell you anything?" Molly asked.

Lauren barked a laugh. "They kept talking about customer confidentiality. So I told them the police would be giving them a call. That felt good."

"She might have stayed somewhere and taken a flight this morning," Molly said.

Lauren sighed. "That's what I'm hoping. Thank you so much for calling. I'm about ready to lose my mind with worry."

"I hear you," Molly said. She was beyond worried herself, and the anxiety grew with every hour that Patsy Mae remained missing. "Let's touch base later, okay?" A group of customers burst through the bakehouse door, chattering and laughing. She was going to have to hang up, much as she hated to.

"It sounds busy there," Lauren said. "I'll let you go. And again, thank you."

For the next few hours, the bakehouse was hectic enough that Molly was able to put her worries aside. She had to focus on preparing hot drinks, serving baked goods, and keeping the service station stocked. The beautiful weather was bringing people to Loch Mallaig, and she overheard discussions about fishing, camping, and hiking—and Reg Tod.

While clearing a table, she caught the conversation between two couples. "They're searching for him over in Ironwood," one man said. "They're almost positive it was him who went to that convenience store."

"As long as he stays far away from here," a woman said with a shudder.

"I can't believe he would do something so sloppy," the second man said. "Why show your face in a place that definitely has cameras?"

Why indeed, Molly wondered. Every move so far had shown keen intelligence. Most people wouldn't have been able to elude the police successfully for a day, let alone even longer. Reg was slipping around the UP like a shadow.

The other woman at the table, who had been checking her phone, gave a loud cackle. "You won't *believe* this. Reg Tod is Gregory Gregg's brother."

"No way," her friend said with a gasp. She leaned closer. "Let me see." After a second, she wrinkled her nose. "Yeah, they look sort of alike. But Gregory was so much more handsome. I had such a crush." She darted a glance at her male companion to see if he was listening, but he was deeply absorbed in a conversation with the other man about fishing.

Unsettled, Molly picked up the bus pan and hurried off to the kitchen. The cat was out of the bag now, and if anything, the news would only fuel the manhunt. While the connection between Reg and Caroline was unclear, the fact he was Gregory's brother and had been in his suite the day he died was pretty incriminating.

How long would Reg be able to continue evading the police? She supposed it would depend on whether or not he made another mistake.

Carol was working at a prep table when Molly entered the kitchen. "The twin thing is all over the news," Carol said.

"I know." Molly set the bus pan on the counter by the dishwasher. "Customers are talking about it."

Bridget began unloading the pan and rinsing mugs with the sprayer. "I wonder what it was like for Reg, growing up in his gorgeous brother's shadow."

"I don't know," Molly said. "But something went wrong in that household. A neighbor told us that Gregory, real name Roger, was estranged from his family for years."

"So sad," Bridget said. "Sometimes we assume celebrities have it made. But obviously that isn't true."

"You can say that again," Carol put in.

"Oh, guess what?" Bridget said. "I'm going to the ball tonight." Her pretty face glowed with happiness. "Neil called and asked me. He was sorry since it was such short notice, but I said it didn't matter. We're friends, so who cares about it being last minute?"

Carol raised an eyebrow at Molly as though she didn't quite believe the pair were just friends, but Molly suppressed an answering grin. Instead, she said, "That's wonderful. We'll see you there."

For the first time that day, Molly's thoughts went to the evening ahead. Like any formal event, it would require extensive primping, including a long bath, full makeup, and a pretty hairstyle. If all went well, dining and dancing with friends would provide refreshment and relaxation, which she definitely could use right now. But she couldn't help wishing that one of the friends joining her would be the still-absent Patsy Mae.

***

Molly was putting the finishing touches on her hair when someone honked outside, and rather insistently at that. Her dress rustling as she moved, she went to the front window to peek out. Angus came too, stretching to prop his feet on the sill.

What was this? A stretch limo was parked in the bakehouse lot, engine purring. Molly opened the window as a uniformed man stepped out from the driver's seat. He lifted his hat to Molly, then opened the rear door.

Fergus. As he emerged, handsome in his formal wear, the sunroof slid open and Carol's excited face appeared.

"Come on down," Carol said, waving.

Fergus bowed. "Your chariot awaits, milady." A mischievous smile crinkled his eyes.

Molly burst into laughter. "I'll be right there," she called. "Give me a minute." Picking up her skirt, she ran into the bedroom to put on her shoes, grab a wrap and her bag, and pause for one last look at her pink gown. She smiled at herself, unable to remember the last time she'd felt this pretty.

"What a treat," Molly said a few minutes later as she settled into a wide, soft seat inside the limo. Besides Carol and Harvey, Laura, Hamish, and Joyce were there, everyone gorgeous in their evening wear.

"I thought we needed a little fun," Fergus said as the limo set off. He poured Molly a glass of sparkling cider and handed it to her, then clinked his glass with hers. "To a wonderful night."

Molly decided to let go of her concerns and worries and just enjoy the moment. "To a wonderful night," she responded.

They didn't go directly to the resort. Instead, the driver took them on a ride around the lake. At a height of land, they stopped and Fergus pulled out a large picnic basket. Inside were cheese and crackers, fresh fruit, and crudités—nibbles that were easy to eat while standing outside and gazing at the loch. The view included the resort and the golf course's patches of emerald green, as well as the cluster of buildings in downtown Loch Mallaig.

Molly pulled her silky wrap a little tighter against the breeze. What a beautiful evening. She could see a line of cars pulling into the resort lot. People were starting to arrive for the ball, which had been opened to the public. Tickets were benefiting a children's charity.

"Cheese and crackers?" the driver asked, holding out a tray.

"Sure, thank you," she said, selecting a piece of brie. She took a bite of soft, mild cheese and crisp, peppery cracker, loving the juxtaposition of textures and flavors.

Fergus came to stand beside her. "It's fun getting a bird's-eye view, isn't it?" He pointed out some landmarks around town, even the bakehouse, which was nestled among trees on the other side of the water.

Slim columns of smoke rose here and there along the lake, either campfires or wood fires burning in fireplaces. Second homeowners were already opening their camps and cabins for the season. Many were tucked deep among the trees, with only a glimpse of roof visible or a glint of glass or metal touched by the sun.

"That place is a sad story," Fergus said, pointing to what had to be a barn set in a tiny field surrounded by thick pines. "The house burned down a few years ago. It used to be a farm, but as you can see, it's all grown over." Judging by the barn's leaning stance, it would soon fall down, the encroaching forest removing every trace of its existence.

"That's too bad," Molly said. A fishing boat buzzed across the glassy, deep blue water, reminding her of Reg, who had hidden in the old boathouse. "Do you really think Reg is on the other side of the

UP?" she asked Fergus. The breeze had intensified and she shivered.

Fergus put an arm around her shoulders. "That's what the police say. I'm sure he's long gone. He must have realized how risky it was to hang around here."

"I hope you're right," Molly said, drawing comfort from Fergus's warmth and reassuring words. "Now if Patsy Mae would show up, everything would be fine."

The cooling air and the time ticking away forced the reluctant revelers away from their impromptu picnic and back into the limo. Their driver continued the circuit they had started around the loch, Harvey and Hamish in rare form as they regaled the group with funny stories. All too soon, they were pulling up the resort driveway and parking under the entrance canopy.

But this was merely the beginning of the evening, Molly realized as Fergus helped her to disembark from the limo. Next was dinner, then dancing. The night was young. And maybe she wasn't, but she still knew how to savor the moment.

The ballroom had been decorated for the event with rose-covered arbors, flowers on all the tables, and draping garlands crisscrossing the ceiling. The tables were set with white linen and candles, and silverware and glasses glinted in the soft light.

In an interesting touch, an employee announced each group's arrival at the entrance to the ballroom. The guests were circulating, pausing in groups to chat while enjoying predinner appetizers. In one corner, an elegant harpist strummed a tall harp.

"Please excuse me, fair lady," Fergus said with a little bow. "I have to check in with my staff."

"Please do," Molly said with a laugh. "I'll see you later."

"Save me a seat." Then with a smile, he was gone, whisking through the throng.

Molly watched him stride across the room, his head held high, pausing to greet friends and guests. Maybe she and Fergus were simply under the spell of this magical evening, but for some reason she felt something had changed between them. Her heart began to beat faster at the thought. Was she imagining things? She certainly hoped not, because if so, she was far too old to make a fool of herself.

Laura put a hand on Molly's arm. "Do you want to come talk to Joe and Alyssa with me?" she asked. She tipped her chin toward where the pair stood on the sidelines. "Maybe they've heard from Patsy Mae."

"Good point," Molly said. "Sure, let's go." Joe wanted to publish Patsy Mae's book, so maybe they'd talked over the past day or so. The last time Molly had checked her phone, there had been no update from Lauren saying that her mother had been in touch—or better yet, arrived home.

"Good evening," Laura said when they reached Joe and Alyssa. "Doesn't the ballroom look wonderful tonight?"

"It certainly does," Joe readily agreed, giving them an embarrassed smile when his companion didn't even glance up from her phone. He gave them a slight bow. "And you're both lovely." He was in formal Highland dress, and Molly was glad to see he'd procured another kilt from somewhere.

"Thank you," Molly said. "It's fun to dress up." She took a breath then asked, "Have you heard from Patsy Mae? It's disappointing that she isn't with us tonight."

Joe appeared taken aback. "She left? She didn't say anything to me about that when I saw her yesterday." He smiled. "I'll be in touch with her a lot over the next few months. One of my favorite things is shepherding a new author into print." Then his eyes sharpened. "What do you mean, heard from her? Is something wrong?"

"We're not sure," Laura said. "We do know that she left the resort around five o'clock yesterday afternoon, but no one has heard from her since."

The editor rubbed his chin. "That is very strange. I hope she's all right."

Beside him, Alyssa gave a sharp exclamation. "That woman will be the death of me!"

"Patsy Mae?" Molly asked, startled.

Alyssa shook her head in a short, sharp movement. "No, Madelaine." She spoke between gritted teeth. "She's giving me fits. The first draft of her last book was not up to snuff, and she's been dragging her feet on the revisions." She waved her phone at them. "And now she's stopped answering my messages."

"Maybe she's busy getting ready," Joe said. "You know how Madelaine loves to get dressed up."

Again Alyssa shook her head, resembling an impatient horse shaking her mane. "That's not it. I was there while the beauticians were working on her. All she had to do is slip on her gown and shoes. No, she's just being difficult."

A note of warning chimed in Molly's ears. "Is it possible she changed her mind about coming to the ball?" she asked tentatively, though she was pretty sure she already knew the answer.

Alyssa's response validated her thoughts. "Madelaine miss an event? Especially one where she is the guest of honor?" She threw her head back and laughed. "There's only one reason Madelaine would miss an appearance in the spotlight." She laughed again. "And that's if she was physically unable to attend."

Laura's eyes went wide, which indicated that she was thinking along the same lines as Molly.

Joe was a beat behind, but he quickly caught on. "I think we'd better go see if Madelaine is all right," he said, urgency in his tone.

Molly, Laura, and Joe hustled across the ballroom, Molly keeping an eye out for Fergus. Unfortunately, she didn't see him anywhere in the vast room, nor in the corridors or lobby.

At the bank of elevators, Joe pushed the up button. "I hope we're overreacting," he said. "But under the circumstances . . ." He didn't need to finish the sentence.

The elevator came quickly. They stepped inside and were whisked up to the third floor, surrounded by a thick, anxious silence.

"She's down this way," Joe said, gesturing for them to follow as he set off at a trot. This was the same floor where Patsy Mae and Caroline had stayed, but she was at the opposite end, closer to Gregory's suite.

Molly was winded by the time they reached the suite. Although her skirt was full, the bodice of her gown was fitted and very restrictive.

Even the athletic Laura was breathing heavily. "I'm glad we don't dress like this every day," she whispered to Molly as Joe began to knock.

"Madelaine?" Joe called, then leaned close to the door. He knocked again, louder this time, and listened. "She's either not in there or something is wrong."

Despite her lack of breath, Molly dashed for the closest house-phone. "I'm calling the desk. We can't take any chances." Could this be happening for a *third* time, that someone was unresponsive in a room and she was the one who discovered them? She groaned softly, praying that Madelaine was all right. "We need someone on the third floor to unlock a room," she told the clerk. "Madelaine Alt is not responding."

They paced the carpet, waiting for someone to come up with a master key. Joe broke the silence. "I just remembered something Patsy Mae said." Molly and Laura looked at him in inquiry. "She said she planned to drive around and take pictures for her next book before she left town. She thought the loch was a perfect inspiration."

This added a whole new twist to Patsy Mae's situation. "Is it possible she never left town?" Molly asked slowly. Horror began to prickle at the back of her neck.

Footsteps sounded on the carpet, and Fergus marched around the corner. Tension etched every line of his grim face as he moved past them to unlock the suite door.

He turned the handle and pushed it open. "Madelaine?" he called. "This is Fergus MacGregor. I'm coming in."

Silence met his announcement.

"Wait here," Fergus ordered. He strode inside, and Molly heard him calling out again. Within less than a minute, he returned to the doorway. "She's not here."

Molly reeled at this news. Was it good—or the opposite?

19

Molly tried to think logically. If Madelaine wasn't in her room or in the ballroom, perhaps she was somewhere else on the grounds, choosing to stay out of touch with her editor.

"What now?" Joe asked. "Start searching for her?"

Fergus made sure the door was secure. "I suppose so. No sense in raising an alarm yet. She's probably wandering around someplace with no idea that people are worried."

Laura crossed her arms. "You'd think she'd know better in times like these," she fumed.

Most people would, Molly reflected. But she had the feeling that Madelaine marched to one drum—her own. "Why don't we check the ballroom again before we start searching the resort? Maybe she's downstairs now and this was a false alarm."

The little group remained silent as they made their way to the elevator. Soon they were back on the main floor and entering the ballroom. Molly stopped to talk to the staff member who had been announcing everyone.

"Excuse me," she said. "Have you seen Madelaine Alt? She's the guest of honor." Molly pointed to a nearby poster of Madelaine on an easel.

The man eyed the poster before nodding. "I sure did. She came in a little bit ago."

"Oh, I am so glad to hear that," Molly said, relief making her knees weak. One down, one to go. In a minute, she'd check in with Lauren and see if Patsy Mae had returned yet.

Fergus's phone buzzed, and he answered it. He spoke tersely for a moment then said to Molly, "I'm so sorry, but I've got to excuse myself. There's an emergency at the golf lodge. Broken pipes."

"Oh no," Molly said, seeing her vision of the evening dissolve like smoke. "I hope you won't be gone too long."

He smiled down into her face. "I'll do my best. Promise you'll save me at least one dance?"

"Of course," Molly said, unable to restrain a giggle of delight. What was wrong with her? She was acting like a teenager.

Fortunately, Fergus didn't seem to mind. "See you soon."

A trumpet fanfare rang out over the sound system, announcing that dinner was to be served. Molly, Laura, and Joe hurried into the ballroom. Joe split off to join Alyssa, and Molly and Laura sat with Carol and their other friends.

Servers began to wheel carts around the room, placing plates of salad in front of the diners. Molly scanned the tables for Madelaine. The woman, with her tall stature, dominant personality, and distinctive sense of style, was usually easy to spot. But Molly didn't see her anywhere. Maybe she'd stepped out to the restroom, Molly mused as she ate her salad.

But by the time the server had cleared her salad plate and replaced it with a main course, Molly realized the guest of honor had not returned. Neither had poor Fergus. What bad timing for an emergency.

Molly picked at her chicken, uneasiness stealing her appetite. Finally she gave up. She needed to move around before she screamed in frustration. She put her cloth napkin on the table. "I'm going to the ladies' room," she said. "Do you two want to go with me?" She gave Laura and Carol significant glances.

Carol immediately rose. "I was about to suggest that." She bent to give Harvey a peck on the cheek. "See you in a few, darling."

"What's really up, Molly?" Laura asked as the trio bustled across the dining room.

Molly put a finger to her lips then pointed at the door attendant. He was slouched in a chair next to the door, watching the guests eat. She slowed as they reached the double doors, which were propped open.

"Hi again," she said to the man. She waited until he raised his head, recognition dawning in his eyes. "Before dinner, I asked you about Madelaine Alt. But I don't see her anywhere. Are you sure she was here?"

The man stood. "I remember. The lady did come in, but she left again right after with a friend. I have no idea where she is now."

A friend? Alyssa and Joe were still seated at the VIP table, Madelaine's empty chair between them. "What did the friend look like?" Molly asked.

The man shrugged. "He was male. Tall. Dressed in a kilt. That's all I remember."

Carol fished her phone from somewhere within her voluminous gown, then tapped the screen a few times. "Was this him?" She showed the man a recent picture of Reg Tod.

"Yeah, I think so," he said with a nod. "I mean, I really didn't pay too much attention."

A chill raced down Molly's spine. Reg Tod was here, and he was with Madelaine. "Thanks," she said. "We've got to go."

Molly managed to walk calmly out of the ballroom but once beyond the doors, she lifted her skirts and broke into a trot.

"Where are we going?" Laura called behind her.

Realizing that running to nowhere wouldn't help anything, Molly faltered to a halt. "I can't believe it," she said. "While the police are scouring Ironwood for Reg, he sneaked in here and kidnapped Madelaine."

Carol set off with clear purpose. "Let's ask the desk clerks if they've seen anything."

"Great idea," Laura said. "We'll keep an eye out on the way."

They checked the public rooms they passed but there was no sign of the pair. In the lobby, Molly approached the desk, hoping that she appeared calm and in control, certainly not what she felt at the moment.

"Hi there," she said to the young woman, the same one who had been on duty the other night. "Have you seen our guest of honor, Madelaine Alt?"

The clerk frowned, then her face lightened. "I did. She and one of those male models went that way." She pointed down a corridor.

So they were still in the building. "Thanks," Molly said. "Have a good night."

As the Bakehouse Three hurried off, the young woman called, "Did you ever catch up with your friend?"

It took Molly a second to realize she was talking about Patsy Mae. "Not yet," Molly said. "But thanks for asking."

"Patsy Mae is still missing?" Carol whispered as they crossed the lobby. "How strange."

"Yes," Laura said. "And get this: Joe Byers said that she was going to drive around Loch Mallaig before heading out of town to get inspiration for her books."

Carol got the implication immediately, her eyes widening. "Maybe she never left town."

"That's what I think," Molly said as they reached the bank of elevators. "And that is another reason why I want to catch up to Reg Tod. Maybe he knows where Patsy Mae is." She glanced around. "Now where? Would they have gone up to Madelaine's room?"

Carol gnawed at her bottom lip. "I doubt it. It would have to be somewhere Reg is comfortable."

Laura pointed to the stairwell. "How about the basement? That's the usual lair of handymen, right?"

Molly hadn't been in that area of the building, but Fergus had told her that it contained access to hotel systems plus storage areas and workshops. Systems like heating and cooling—and water. She couldn't restrain an exclamation. "Remember that emergency Fergus went to? I wonder if Reg sabotaged the water pipes at the golf club."

"That would create a wonderful diversion," Laura noted. She pushed on the staircase door. "Coming?"

Carol frowned. "Shouldn't we tell someone first?"

"There are three of us and one of him," Laura argued. "We'll be fine. Plus, we don't even know if anything is wrong."

"But if it is," Molly said. "We need to hurry. Madelaine could be . . ." She swallowed hard, unable to force the words past the lump in her throat.

"Send Fergus a text," Carol told Molly. "At least he'll know where we are."

"I will," Molly said. She shot off a short message to Fergus, but didn't wait for a reply. He was probably up to his knees in water.

Laura opened the stairwell door. "Be very quiet," she whispered. "We don't want to give Reg any warning that we're coming." She carefully pulled the door shut behind them.

They held up their skirts and descended the concrete stairs, trying not to make too much noise with their dress shoes. Down to the landing, then down again to the bottom floor of the hotel. A metal door with a wired-glass window lay ahead. Beyond it was darkness.

"That's strange," Molly said. "Why are the lights not on down here?"

Carol opened the door. "Maybe they use motion-sensitive lighting. It saves energy."

As the three slipped through into a wide hallway, though, the overhead lights remained off. Lines of doors extended on either side, all of them closed. The corridor was pitch-dark, only the lighted stairwell behind them providing any illumination.

Carol reached for a bank of switches and flicked them up and down. "They're not working."

A cold wave of dread washed over Molly. This was confirmation that Reg was down here somewhere and had disconnected the lights. Fergus would never allow such an unsafe situation.

"We need some light," Laura whispered. "It's not safe to stumble around in the dark." She found her phone and switched it on. "I'll keep it low so we don't warn Reg that we're coming."

Laura shielded the light with her hand, providing enough glow that they could see to place their feet. Huddled together, they trod quietly along the hall.

On they went, past doors labeled *Laundry, Paper Goods,* and *Dishware.* Molly pictured the contents of the closets, shelves stacked with goods, washing machines and dryers quiet now but ready for service in the morning.

The hum of air-conditioning equipment and the sound of water rushing through the pipes told Molly they were approaching the systems area of the basement. Here were all the controls that fed air and water and heat to the rooms above. Reg's stomping ground.

"What's that?" Carol grabbed Molly's arm. "I thought I heard a voice."

The trio halted and listened, ears straining. The cooling equipment shut off briefly and Molly distinctly heard a woman shouting, although the words weren't distinguishable. A man's deep voice replied, his words also hard to make out.

"Down there," she said, pointing. Running on tiptoe, the three continued, reaching a huge room that held the heating and cooling system. A light shone on the floor in a far corner, a small and steady glow like that of a lantern. Reg had come prepared.

This light, although limited, provided enough illumination for them to make their way across the floor without bumping into the heavy air-conditioning units and ducts. Once they reached the other side, they paused near the open doorway to listen, careful to stay out of view.

"Just think," the man said. "Everyone is waiting upstairs for the guest of honor. Don't you want to join them?" He sounded like Reg, Molly thought, although she wasn't totally sure.

The response was a cackle of glee. "My ego isn't that big," Madelaine said. "And I'm not that stupid. I'm certainly not going to confess to you just so I can go and make a speech." Another cackle. "Seriously, Reg, you are demented, and you need to let me go. Now."

"*I'm* demented?" Reg's tone was low and forbidding. "You're the one who killed my brother."

20

Molly clapped a hand over her mouth to muffle an involuntary gasp. Madelaine was the killer, not Reg. Or so he believed—enough to lurk around the resort, kidnap Madelaine, and try to force a confession out of her.

"Why would I kill Gregory?" Madelaine's tone indicated a sneer painted her face. "He was the best cover model we had. My fans all loved him."

"I wondered that myself," Reg said. "It didn't make sense to me. But then I saw the Isla Tod manuscript in Caroline's room and put two and two together." He paused dramatically. "He was writing your books for you, wasn't he? I recognized his style in your last two or three. When we were younger, I was the only one who knew his love of writing, and I always read his work and gave him feedback. His voice was subtle, but easy to pick up once you know what to look for. What a shame your talent seems to have run out."

Madelaine used Gregory as a ghostwriter? Molly thought back to Alyssa's argument with him. Had Gregory decided to stop writing books for Madelaine? That would explain why Alyssa was so upset. She wouldn't want her top author's career to fail because she had a case of writer's block. And sooner or later, as book quality declined, it would.

Madelaine laughed again, but it sounded hollow now. "Maybe you should start writing novels, Reg. You have a gift for fiction."

"And so did my brother." His tone turned musing. "How odd it was to see a manuscript by Isla Tod in Caroline's room. Isla Tod was my great-grandmother, and you must admit that is a very unusual name. I'll bet Caroline wanted to represent Gregory as his agent."

The author's response was a screech of hatred. "That witch. Selling me out. She didn't care if my career tanked while she built him up. I've sold millions of books, made Caroline's career as an agent, but she seemed to forget that. She sold Gregory's book behind my back, without even a courtesy heads-up."

Molly wondered which publishing company had bought the book. Even if she wasn't quite confessing, Madelaine had revealed a definite motive for both murders.

"I'm sure you're tired of sitting down here," Reg said. "So why don't we get this over with? Let me record a confession and I'll release you."

"A coerced confession won't be worth anything," Madelaine said. "Don't you know that?"

"But I'll know. It's why I ran away when that manuscript I went back and took from Caroline's room made me a suspect, why I hid and messed with the security cameras and waited for a chance to get you alone. I want to be able to lay my brother to rest." Reg made a strangled sound and Molly realized he was sobbing. "The regret I feel for not reconnecting with him sooner after our parents died is something I have to live with the rest of my life. A tiny fight they had grew into an irreparable rift, and I didn't get a chance to—"

"Oh, boo-hoo," Madelaine said. "Your whole life isn't imploding in front of your eyes the way mine did."

"All right," Reg said. "I won't record it. But please, put me out of my misery. Did you kill my brother?"

Madelaine was silent for a long moment. "I did. That man was so vain. I think he used his tanning bed every day to maintain that special glow." Her voice became mocking. "But he was getting older, as we all are. It was only a matter of time before his career as a cover model would be over."

"And that's why he wanted to switch over to being an author," Reg said. "It makes sense."

"But he was doing it at my expense." The ugly tone was back in Madelaine's voice. "I begged him not to, his girlfriend begged him not to, but he wouldn't listen. He said he needed to keep his creative energy for his books."

Understandable, Molly thought. After keeping his efforts under wraps, no doubt Gregory was excited to publish something of his own, even if it was under a pen name.

"So you killed my brother, mere hours after I saw him again after twenty long years." Reg's voice conveyed his utter sadness. "And Caroline too, I assume?"

Madelaine snickered. "Oh yeah. And I have to admit enjoying that one. I even toyed with her a little first, sending her that nasty note. She was so arrogant. I was the talent. I could take a dumb idea from her and turn it into gold, like my last book. Without me, she was nothing, and she knew it."

Molly grimaced, assuming that Madelaine was inadvertently confessing to getting the plot of her book about Queen Margaret's lady-in-waiting from Caroline. *One more mystery solved.*

"How did you kill Caroline?" Reg asked. "I heard she had a reaction to hair dye. Not a typical murder weapon."

"I kept razzing her about how brassy her hair looked." Madelaine's tone was smug. "She dyed it herself, believe it or not—one of her little frugalities, although she was incredibly vain. So it was pretty simple to convince her to try a new color. I told her I'd bought it for myself, but realized it wouldn't work with my skin tone. I insisted she take it, and she did." She giggled. "But there was a little something extra added."

"What was it?" Reg asked. "I wouldn't know where to begin."

"Oh, it was easy," Madelaine bragged. "I used liquid nicotine. Absorbs through the skin and works quickly, especially if you're allergic to it like she was. She had told me about an unfortunate incident in her youth when she'd tried smoking, and how disaster had barely been averted that time." Madelaine gave a nasty laugh. "She never knew what hit her."

Molly exchanged glances with Carol and Laura. Madelaine was definitely a dangerous and ruthless killer. But what would Reg do next? He couldn't exactly set her free. Hopefully the police could find enough evidence to arrest and convict Madelaine before she killed again.

Then Madelaine complained, "Think you could loosen my wrists a little? My circulation is getting cut off. I already have arthritis in my hands."

Something told Molly that getting too close to Madelaine was a bad move on Reg's part, but before she could shout a warning, Reg hollered and she heard sounds of a struggle.

Without a second thought, Molly ran into the room, Carol and Laura behind her. Madelaine and Reg were struggling for a revolver Reg held. Blood dripped from a scratch down Reg's arm. A long and lethal hatpin lay on the floor, along with Madelaine's feathered hat.

Together the Bakehouse Three tackled Madelaine, pulling her off Reg. It took almost all of Molly's energy to restrain the flailing woman, who was stronger than she appeared. Madelaine kicked out with one leg, almost hitting Molly, who had to jump aside.

"Cut it out," Laura warned. "There are three of us and one of you."

The handyman gazed up at them in amazement. "Where did you come from?"

"Never mind that right now," Carol told him. "Help us tie her up again."

Reg picked up the rope that had been binding Madelaine's wrists.

"Take it easy," Molly said. "We don't want to hurt you."

Madelaine struggled a bit more but finally gave up, going so limp they had to prop her up. Another trick.

"You're a crafty one," Carol said as she held Madelaine's arm so Reg could tie the rope.

"I've written lots of books," the author snarled. "And my heroes and heroines have escaped far worse situations than this many, many times." Her face lit up in fiendish glee. "You may have stopped me, but there is something you aren't going to stop."

"What do you mean?" Molly asked. Had Madelaine set another trap for someone?

"Alyssa Martin," Madelaine said between clenched teeth. "She was going to publish Isla Tod. *Et tu, Brute?*"

"What did you do, Madelaine?" Molly demanded. They needed to save Alyssa. She hoped it wasn't too late.

Footsteps thundered in the corridor, giving Molly a jolt of hope. Help was on the way.

"Alyssa is vain too," Madelaine said. "So vain. How many selfies does one person need?" She shook her head, an evil smile on her lips.

That was all Molly needed. Alyssa's phone had been rigged somehow to hurt her.

Fergus burst into the room, followed by Harvey and a couple of officers. "Molly! You're all right."

"She is, and so are we," Carol said with a smile at Harvey. She released Madelaine's arm. "You might want to talk to these two." As the officers moved toward Reg, she added, "Reg is innocent. Madelaine Alt is the killer."

"We heard it all," Laura told Fergus and the others, who appeared stunned at this news. "She killed Gregory and Caroline."

"And she's going to kill Alyssa." Molly pushed past the newcomers. "We need to go find her right now."

Molly picked up her skirts and ran, thankful that Fergus had figured out how to turn on the corridor lights again. Clacking footsteps told her that Laura and Carol were right behind her. The doors to the staff elevator stood open now, so she dashed inside and, after waiting for the other two, pushed the button for the first floor. With a hum, the elevator began to rise.

"Last time I saw Alyssa, she was sitting with Joe Byers," Molly managed between heavy breaths. "I hope she's still there and nothing has happened yet." Not only had Molly been moving at top speed, but her chest was tight with anxiety. Would they make it in time?

"How can you kill someone with their cell phone?" Carol asked. "I gather that's what she was implying."

"I don't know," Laura said. "But if she spent half that ingenuity on her books instead of rigging things to kill people, she never would have needed a ghostwriter."

The effort criminals put into their malevolent pursuits often amazed Molly as well. How far might they get in life if they applied that energy to something productive?

The elevator doors opened with a ding and the three women rushed out in a bunch. They were at the end of a corridor in the area of the hotel reserved for employees.

"Which way?" Molly asked.

"This way." Without hesitation, Laura set off through a maze of corridors, and soon they emerged into the lobby.

"You have a great sense of direction," Carol said in admiration.

"Not exactly," Laura said with a modest shrug. "I've used the staff elevator once or twice to make deliveries."

Molly almost bypassed the front desk, then thought better of it and stopped. "Have you seen Alyssa Martin tonight?" she asked the clerk. "Is she still in the ballroom?"

The young woman frowned in confusion. "I think so. Everyone is in there."

Not everyone, but Molly didn't quibble. "Thank you."

They kept going toward the ballroom, passing a few people coming the other way. Dinner was definitely over.

Molly burst through the ballroom doors and scanned the room. Some people were standing in groups talking while others sat at tables with their dessert and coffee. Servers were clearing the buffet and carting away dirty dishes.

Where is Alyssa? Molly started making a circuit of the ballroom. Her heart lurched when she finally spotted the editor standing next to Joe, who had his arm around her. They were smiling at a woman who was holding a phone, preparing to take a picture.

Preparing to take a picture? Molly leaped across the carpet in several great bounds, her arm flying out and snatching the phone out of the woman's hand.

"Hey!" the woman shouted. "What are you doing?"

Molly didn't bother to answer. Instead she tossed the phone into a nearby bowl of pink punch, recently replenished by a server.

Alyssa shrieked, her hands going to her face. "That's my brand-new phone!"

A muffled thump sounded against the side of the bowl, followed by a geyser of pink liquid shooting upward. Anything within a three-foot radius was drenched in a blast of sticky punch—an explosion that had been intended for Alyssa Martin.

21

Nearby onlookers screamed as they ducked.

"What was that?" one woman asked.

"It was a bomb!" a man answered.

"I'm covered in punch," another woman complained, her nose wrinkled in distaste. "Yuck."

Carol and Laura hurried up to Molly. "Wow," Laura said. "That was scary."

"I'll say." Carol gave Molly a quick hug. "How brave of you to do that."

Molly shuddered as her adrenaline ebbed. "I'm glad I got to her in time. It wouldn't have been pretty." She realized the guests around them were beginning to panic. "Excuse me a second."

Putting two fingers in her mouth, she whistled, a piercing sound that cut through the excited chatter.

Once things quieted, she projected her voice loud and clear. "Everything is all right, folks. Someone rigged the cell phone to blow up, but the liquid muffled the explosion." She waved her arms at the crowd. "Go about your business."

"Blow up?" Alyssa swayed on her feet and Joe rushed to prop her up, then help her to a nearby chair. "But who? Why?"

Neil appeared at Molly's elbow. "I need you to tell me what's going on," he murmured in a low but urgent voice. Then louder, he called out, "Please, everyone. Do what Molly said. As you were." He gestured to the musicians waiting to play and they struck up a lively tune. After a few bars of that, guests began to mill about again.

Molly gazed at Neil. "Do you know they're arresting Madelaine Alt for murder right about now?" She pointed at the floor. "Down in the basement."

He ran a hand through his hair, a gesture so like his father that Molly felt a pang. "No, I've been in the kitchen supervising the meal. Last I heard, Dad was at the golf club. Something about a water leak."

"That was a diversion, I believe," Molly said, starting toward Alyssa. Neil followed. "Reg Tod came back to the resort to squeeze a confession out of Madelaine. He figured out that she killed his brother and Caroline."

"We heard the whole thing," Laura said, flanking Molly on one side. Carol walked beside Neil on the other.

They arrived at the table where Alyssa sat, pale faced. Molly gave her the overview about Madelaine's guilt. "You were next. She told us she did something to your phone."

Joe exclaimed in horror and disbelief. "I can't wrap my mind around this at all. Why would Madelaine hurt Alyssa? Alyssa was her editor."

Molly studied the young woman, who had her head bowed. "You know why, don't you, Alyssa? You were going to publish Isla Tod's book."

Alyssa bit her lip and nodded. "I didn't have a choice. It was bad enough that Gregory was refusing to ghostwrite any more, but I knew if I wanted him to stay with me, I'd have to show him I valued his talent." She shuddered. "And I do—did. I assumed Madelaine would be angry, but I never guessed she'd do anything like this." Sobs made her shoulders heave as she covered her face with both hands.

A server had moved toward the punch bowl, peering curiously at the cell phone lying in the bottom.

Neil held up a hand. "Don't touch that," he ordered, striding over. "We need to get the police in here." He and the server picked up the table and moved it out of the way.

"There's one more thing," Molly said to Carol and Laura. "Patsy Mae. We need to ask Reg Tod if he saw her." She glanced around the ballroom. "I think we can leave this to Neil, don't you?"

"Absolutely," Laura said. "We'd better go intercept the police before they take Reg to the station."

Once again, the trio rushed out of the ballroom, this time on a mission to find their missing friend. In the lobby, they found the police leading a handcuffed Madelaine Alt through, and a deflated Reg with them. Now that Molly got a good look, she saw that he was wearing Joe's kilt, which had helped him blend in with the crowd. He was also clearly exhausted, and no wonder after days of working to bring his brother's killer to justice.

Molly spotted Fergus talking to the chief. "Fergus," she called, and he turned. "I have a question for Reg. Oh, and Madelaine, you'll be happy to know we managed to get Alyssa's cell phone away from her before it exploded. You won't be charged with a third murder here, but there is punch everywhere."

Madelaine shrieked with fury.

"Good job, Molly," Fergus said. "Where is the cell phone now?"

"In the bottom of a punch bowl, waiting to be taken into evidence," Molly replied. She smiled at the chief's bewildered expression. "I'll give you a statement, Chief, but right now we need to find out where Patsy Mae Wallace is. We think Reg might know."

The chief's eyes sharpened. "The missing woman from Louisiana? Why do you believe he knows where she is?"

"Because I think he was driving her rental car when he led you all on a wild goose chase," Molly said. "He wasn't in his truck. And Joe Byers told us that Patsy Mae was taking a drive around the loch before leaving."

"She's right," Reg said. "Patsy Mae is at the old Pendleton farm.

The house is gone, so I've been camping in the barn since my hidey-hole in the boathouse got busted."

"Is that the place we saw from the overlook?" Molly asked Fergus. To think that was only a couple of hours ago. While they were staring at the old place, they'd been totally unaware that it was Reg's hideout.

"Did you hurt Patsy Mae?" Laura demanded. "You better not have."

The handyman shook his head. "No, I didn't lay a hand on her, except to keep her from running off. She happened upon me, and I couldn't let her leave." His expression was mournful. "I'm so, so sorry. She's a nice woman." His lips lifted briefly. "She told me she was going to consider it research for her next book."

Molly couldn't suppress a laugh. Patsy Mae was amazing. "Let's go get her, ladies."

Harvey put up a hand. "I don't know about this. Carol, you already put yourself at risk once tonight."

"But the bad guy is right here," Carol said. "Reg, is anyone else at the farm?"

He shook his head. "No, I've been working alone."

"An officer needs to go with you," Chief Thomson said. "Anderson, please accompany these women."

Fergus stepped closer to Molly. "I'd love to come along, but there is so much going on here right now."

Molly patted his arm. "You're needed here. We'll be back right away." She crossed her fingers that Patsy Mae really was fine. "See you soon?"

His blue eyes crinkled in a smile. "You bet. I'll be watching for you."

Harvey wanted to go, but Greer didn't have room for him in the cruiser, so he stayed behind to help in any way he could.

Realizing that they wouldn't be able to fit everyone in the squad car if they did find Patsy Mae, the women stopped briefly at Laura's nearby cottage to retrieve her Beetle. Carol rode with Laura while Molly sat in the front seat of the cruiser. Greer led the way, saying she knew the way to the Pendleton farm since the site had long been a lure for vandals and teens. From Laura's, Greer drove away from town to wind along the loch.

They were passing a stretch of woods when Greer pulled over and braked.

"I can't even see the driveway," Molly said, staring into the underbrush, which appeared unbroken to a casual eye.

"I suppose that's why it's such a great hideout," Greer said.

With Laura still behind them, they bumped along the old lane, bushes and brambles brushing against the car. After a short distance, Greer stopped and pointed to a wire cable stretched across the driveway. "I'm going to check that out."

Greer got out and examined the wire. From her body language, Molly gathered that it had been cut and then temporarily attached to fool the casual viewer.

The officer returned to the cruiser and proceeded. A couple of minutes later, they emerged into a clearing. Molly could tell by the age of the forest that much larger fields had once surrounded the house and barn. The house was nothing but a cellar hole, as Fergus had said. But the barn still stood, though it listed a bit to one side, the roof covered in moss and the walls water stained. The loch could be glimpsed through the trees, and Molly realized that at one time, this had been a beautiful property.

Officer Anderson parked the cruiser and climbed out, Molly joining her. Laura pulled to one side, but as she and Carol started to get out, the officer gestured for the Bakehouse Three to wait while she approached the barn. First Greer tugged on the main door, which didn't budge, then she circled the barn to find another way inside.

Molly clenched her fists, her fingernails biting into her palms. What if Patsy Mae wasn't all right? *What if . . . ?* She couldn't bring herself to finish the sentence, even in her mind.

As if reading her thoughts, Laura said, "Remember, Reg isn't a killer. He made serious errors in judgment, yes, but he didn't hurt anyone."

"We think," Carol said, her face creased in distress. "Oh, please let Patsy Mae be okay."

After what seemed like an interminable time, the front barn door slid open with a squeal of rusty old wheels. Greer stood in the doorway, and beside her was Patsy Mae. She was dressed in rumpled clothing, smudges on her face and hay in her hair, but she looked whole and healthy.

The trio burst forward, running toward their friend. "Can we hug her?" Carol asked the officer. At Greer's nod, they gathered Patsy Mae into a group embrace. Her clothes held the aroma of woodsmoke, but other than that, she was the same old Patsy Mae.

"Now that's what I call a greeting," Patsy Mae said. "Thanks for coming to get me. After Reg took off this afternoon, I thought he might never come back." She grinned. "I was getting ready to claw my way out if I had to."

Officer Anderson was on her phone, speaking to the chief. When she returned to the little group, she said, "An ambulance is coming to check you out, Mrs. Wallace. And a crime scene team. The chief wants me to take a statement if you're up for it right now."

"Whatever it takes so I can get home," Patsy Mae said, tears springing to her eyes. "My poor kids must be frantic."

"They are." Molly handed Patsy Mae her cell phone. "Give Lauren a call, and then we want to hear what happened." She glanced at Greer to see if there was an objection, but she merely nodded.

Patsy Mae placed the call. "I'm fine, sweet pea," she said after giving a brief summary of her experience. "I went for a drive and turned down the wrong driveway, that's all. No, he didn't hurt me. But he couldn't let me go. He told me that he was being framed for his brother's murder. He'd gotten a job at the resort knowing he could get in touch with Gregory at the convention, and their brief reunion made it all the more painful when he was killed. So, Reg said he was going to get a confession out of the real killer. And guess what? I believed him."

"The killer has been arrested," Molly said. "Madelaine Alt." Officer Anderson frowned, so Molly added, "*Alleged* killer."

"So, I spent the time plotting out another book," Patsy Mae said. "Reg was good enough to take notes for me. My hands were tied, you see."

Patsy Mae had put her daughter on speaker, and they could all hear Lauren's exclamation. "Mom, you are something else. Who plots a book while they're being held captive?"

Patsy Mae laughed. "I guess I do. Everything a writer encounters is grist for the mill, right? I guess I'm really good at using my experiences for inspiration." She shrugged. "Plus it was really boring once I realized Reg wasn't going to hurt me."

Molly had no doubt that her friend was going to be a huge success. How could she fail? Not only was she incredibly talented, she had the spirit and heart of a lion.

"Anyway, I've got to go, sweet pea," Patsy Mae said. "They're going to check me over and take my statement. I'll be home tomorrow."

"Hold on, Mom," Lauren said. "You're not going anywhere. Jerome and I are on our way to you."

"What?" Patsy Mae's brows skyrocketed. "What do you mean?"

"We're at the airport as we speak. After we pick up our rental car, we're coming to Loch Mallaig. We have reservations at the resort."

Patsy Mae burst into tears. "Oh, I'm so happy! I can't wait to see you and your brother." She shook her head. "Why ever are you coming here?"

"We were going to search for you, Mom," Lauren replied tearily. "Every square inch of the Upper Peninsula if we had to."

Molly tipped her head toward Laura's car. It was time to go and allow Officer Anderson to do her job. The sooner she started, the sooner Patsy Mae could get back to the resort and see her children. If they were at the airport now, it would be another hour or more before they arrived. Surely the police would be finished with Patsy Mae by then.

"We're going to go," Molly told Greer. "We'll be at the resort if you need us." She lifted her gown. "Now that everything has been solved, maybe we can actually enjoy the dance."

"Thanks for your help," Greer said. "It's been a long, strange few days. And your sharp eyes and tenacity certainly contributed to this positive outcome."

Molly was flattered by the officer's words, especially since she greatly respected Greer. "Thank you. We're so fortunate Loch Mallaig has dedicated officers like you." Molly's heart was bursting with such joy to find Patsy Mae safe that she ignored Greer's uniform and professional demeanor and hugged her tightly. Greer chuckled and returned the embrace.

Carol and Laura also hugged and thanked the officer, then, with promises to see Patsy Mae later, they returned to the Beetle and departed the old farm.

Molly lolled back against the soft back seat. "I'm so happy I could shout and dance a Highland fling."

Carol twisted around in the seat with a smile. "Now we know you are really happy. The Lowlanders are leading some dances tonight. Want to join in?"

Molly laughed. "No thank you. I'll only mess everyone else up." But she would hopefully dance a few ballroom numbers with Fergus. Lost in these happy thoughts, the ride back to the resort passed in a flash.

They stopped by the ladies' room to refresh their hair and wash up. Molly touched up her lipstick, noticing how pink her cheeks were. With all this excitement, she didn't need more makeup to glow.

All had been restored to normal in the ballroom, and dancers were floating about the floor while music played. One couple was Neil and Bridget, and they both waved when they saw Molly and the others.

Harvey hurried out of the crowd and bowed in front of Carol. "May I have this dance, lovely lady?"

Carol laughed. "Of course." She held out her hand to Harvey and he took it, put an arm around her, and whirled her away.

A kilted model came to claim Laura for a dance, leaving Molly alone. But she didn't mind. She was enjoying the moment, the release from tension and fear she'd been laboring under for days. What a huge and enormous relief it was to find the killer and have Patsy Mae restored to them.

She circled the ballroom and, noticing the doors were open to the terrace, slipped outside into the cool evening air. Swathes of stars filled the inky sky and a crescent moon hung low. With every deep breath, Molly inhaled the aroma of roses from the nearby garden. Summer was here.

A tall figure strode out of the dark. As he passed under a lantern, Molly recognized Fergus. He saw her at the same time, and his steps hitched. "Molly. Here you are. I was just catching a breath of fresh air." He laughed. "Clearing my head too, to be honest. What a night."

"What a week," Molly said. She glanced back at the ballroom doors, not ready to go inside. "Do you want to take a stroll? I'd love to walk down to the water." She never got enough of spending time by the lake, a privilege of living in Loch Mallaig.

Fergus held out his arm and Molly put her hand in the crook of his elbow. He pulled it close to his side and they set off, crossing the terrace toward a path.

He knew every inch of the property so Molly let him lead, walking along beside him in perfect contentment. She gazed up at his profile and smiled.

He saw the look. "Molly," he said, his deep voice resonant. "If there's one thing I realize every time you get wrapped up in hunting down a killer, it's that you mean an awful lot to me."

Giddy joy rose in Molly's chest. "What do you know? I feel the exact same way." She tilted her head and said in a teasing voice, "Good thing for you."

He squeezed her hand, throwing her a smile. "A very good thing indeed."